D1578103

HUGO

by *MARIA GRIPE*

WITH DRAWINGS BY
HARALD GRIPE

translated from the Swedish by
Paul Britten Austin
CHATTO & WINDUS
LONDON

Published by
Chatto & Windus Ltd
40–42 William IV Street
London W.C.2

ISBN 0 7011 0298 5

Text © 1966 Maria Gripe
Illustrations © 1966 Harald Gripe
Translation © 1970 Dell Publishing Co., Inc.

Originally published in Sweden under the title
Hugo by Albert Bonniers Forlag, Stockholm.
First published in this edition 1971
Second impression 1975

Printed and bound in Great Britain by
Redwood Burn Limited
Trowbridge & Esher

HUGO

I

"I'M BACK NOW, Miss . . ."

No one even heard the door open. A moment ago all heads were bowed over the exercise books. Now they pop up, and all eyes turn towards the door. Slowly, the teacher lifts her chalk from the blackboard, and says in a low voice:

"So I see . . ."

It's Hugo. Here he is again, with his satchel, his stable lantern, and his bright green braces. He's standing in the doorway, looking at them.

Amazing! You could hear a pin drop! The children sit at their desks, motionless as statues. The teacher, too, stands quite still, her bit of chalk poised in the air. Hugo closes the door behind him.

"Thought it might be time," he says, "to come to school again. So I just strolled over . . ."

No one utters a sound. He slips off his satchel.

". . . so here I am, present again," he adds, as if delivering an important message—which is just what it is for most of them. He has been away an *awfully* long time. Why? No one knows.

No one ever does, with Hugo.

Now he fixes his blue wide-eyed gaze on the teacher and says in a voice that brooks no contradiction:

"*I'm here now.*"

And the teacher replies, as before, in a low voice: "So I see."

Suddenly, as if awaking from a dream, she pulls herself together, turns hastily towards the blackboard, and begins writing up figures. Hugo gives her a look of sympathy and understanding:

"Well," he says, "it's no good falling behind, is it? It's not as if one lived to be a thousand."

The teacher throws him a glance over her shoulder.

"Hugo," she says. "You know where your desk is. Go and sit down." Her voice isn't faint any more.

"Sounds to me," says Hugo, "as if you've got a bone to pick with me, Miss."

She reflects on this a moment, then answers:

"Yes. I should like to know why you've been away from school, Hugo; but that's something we can talk about afterwards."

"Not much to talk about," he says softly. "It's just that they take up such an awful amount of time."

"What on earth are you talking about, Hugo?"

"My water-spiders . . ."

"Oh, I see! So it's water-spiders that have been keeping you away from school week after week?"

"Yes, well. And all the other kinds too, see? But the water-spiders most. They're the ones that take up the most time. You'd be amazed, the time they take up. You think you've been tending to them five minutes, and it turns out to be five hours. Not like in school here, where every minute seems like an hour. It's different with water-spiders, you see, because there's such a lot to *learn* from them."

On the teacher's cheeks two round red roses begin to bloom. Her eyes, too, are quite round.

[3]

"What do you mean, Hugo? Hasn't school anything to teach you?"

Her voice is sharp. She sounds a bit upset. But he calms her:

"No. I don't mean that. School's all right, in its way. But each thing in its turn, see? And spiders can't be expected to follow school rules, can they?"

"I'm not asking them to," says the teacher. "But that *you* obey school rules, Hugo, is something I absolutely insist on."

He looks at her—amazed. She must be joking. What—he, obey school rules?

A deathly silence reigns in the classroom. Everyone is listening breathlessly, though many don't understand what it's all about.

"But . . . when am I to have time to study my animals, then," he persists, calmly, "if I'm to obey school rules?"

"In your spare time, Hugo."

"But . . . that's when I go to school!"

The red spots on the teacher's cheeks get redder. Her hair falls down over her face. She brushes it away.

"We'll talk about this after school, Hugo. Please go and sit down now."

"Thanks," he says. "That'll be nice." He goes over to his seat, the seat next to Josephine's. But it's empty, too. Has the teacher moved her? He looks round the classroom. No, she's not here.

"Where's Josephine?" he asks. "What's she up to?"

Accusingly, he looks from her empty place to the teacher:

"Is she absent?"

The teacher nods.

"Ill?"

"Yes. But she'll be back soon. In this class we aren't usually away more than a couple of days. Not *usually*. Not," she says meaningfully, "for weeks on end."

But Hugo doesn't get it.

"Oh," is all he says. For a while he just sits there, while the teacher goes back to her sums on the blackboard. Then he pipes up again:

"But she's *never* away . . . wonder what it can be . . ."

"Whatever it is, it isn't the spider-sickness," says the teacher. "She'll be back soon. And I don't want to hear another word about it."

"No?"

"No!"

"Oh . . ."

The chalk squeaks on the blackboard. The teacher writes with jerky movements, banging her piece of chalk against the board. Hugo sits lost in thought. After a while he remembers his classmates. He turns round in his seat, waves, nods to right and left. Then, getting up, he goes from one to another.

"Hello, I haven't seen you for ages. How's your grandpa?" He shakes hands and chats.

[5]

Slowly, the teacher turns round.

"I have to mind my manners, you know, being away so long and all," he explains, apologetically.

"Very well. But do hurry up," she says, exhausted. "I thought maybe we'd also have a little time for sums today."

"Of course, there'll be time for that too, Miss. Don't worry . . ."

No, don't worry. She sits down in her chair. She knows all too well what she's in for, and that nothing can stop it.

Hugo goes around the classroom, politely inquiring after the health of uncles and aunts, grandpas and grandmas, discussing the last month's weather and how the harvest is likely to turn out this year. Meanwhile the teacher sits silently waiting.

When he's finished, he goes back to his desk and sits down. The lesson continues. Hugo never meant to interfere—just felt he had to follow his own ideas on how to behave with people, as with animals. But the teacher's lack of respect for water-spiders troubles him.

He looks at her. She writes up sums, adds and subtracts. It's all terribly important to her, he can see that. She's so serious about everything—everything to do with school. He's a little sorry for her, and wonders why.

Suddenly, as he sits there, he begins thinking aloud:

"Trouble with her is, she's been giving too many lessons. She hasn't been out in the woods enough. That's why she bothers so much about all that."

The teacher swings round. She gives a deep sigh. He meets her glance.

"It's a pity. And she's such a nice person, too . . ."

He means what he says. It comes from the heart. No flattery—that's not in his nature. The teacher looks completely lost.

"Hugo, really . . ."

She forgets what she was about to say. She wasn't in the least prepared for his return today, after being absent so long. And Hugo does take some getting used to—the sort who always keeps you on your toes.

Defenceless, she takes flight into her sums. And for a while nothing more is heard from Hugo. But suddenly he is heard yawning. He looks strange. His eyes become shiny. Again and again he puts up a hand to stifle a yawn. Then he apologizes.

"Haven't had a wink of sleep for five nights. What I need is a little nap."

Placing his arms on his desk, he lays his head on them and falls asleep instantly.

Completely at a loss, the teacher looks round.

"Er . . . Hugo's a bit tired," she says, "but he mustn't get cold . . ."

As though she had issued a command, everyone vanishes out into the corridor, grabs coats and scarves. Then they all approach Hugo on tiptoe.

"Ssh . . . don't wake him up!"

"My coat's warmer than yours . . ."

"Mine's got a lamb's-wool lining . . ."

"Mine's got a fur collar . . ."

"That's enough," whispers the teacher. "He doesn't need more than three."

"Shouldn't he have something round his knees?"

"All right. But that's enough . . ."

"His feet are sticking out. Nothing's any good if your feet are cold."

"Ssh, ssh . . ."

"There, now he can't possibly catch cold. That's fine."

The entire class stands round Hugo, looking at him reverently, wrapped up like a bundle of old clothes. Only his tousled hair sticks up. Teacher adjusts the bundle, pats it shyly.

"Spiders must be very tiring," she says.

Suddenly he looks up, out of his bright blue eyes.

"Spiders, no," he says aloud. "They can look after themselves, they're philosophers, you see. But school . . ."

Then he drops off again.

2

WHY IS Josephine staying at home? Wherever she goes, Hans and Gabrielle look at her accusingly. Their eyes are bright with suspicion. Hans and Gabrielle are her grown-up brother and sister. They have children of their own but that doesn't make them a scrap more understanding.

"Are you ill?"

"What's the matter with you, then?"

Josephine shakes her head, doesn't answer.

"Well, then! Why are you at home?"

It's on the tip of her tongue to tell the truth: that Hugo's away and she doesn't *want* to go to school. Then she realizes how silly this would sound. So instead she puts on an expression of silent suffering, heroically borne.

"Got a pain somewhere?"

She nods.

"Where?"

All these questions! All these looks! They make her feel so confused. And she isn't quite quick enough in deciding just where the pain is. Silently, without a word, she holds first her head—then in turn her tummy, ears, throat. Always with the same suffering expression.

"That's a lot of places all at once! I suppose you must be ill, then?"

No. She isn't, she assures them. Not in the least.

"Obviously a hopeless case," says Hans, and shrugs his shoulders, throwing Gabrielle a meaningful glance.

And the battle's lost—lost, that is, for Josephine.

Straight to bed she goes, with a stocking round her neck, one big bandage round her ears, another round her tummy. The stocking tickles dreadfully. It's as if an army of ants were marching round her neck—millions of ants.

"Oh," she gasps, "I'm dying."

"Oh, no you're not! You won't die. But perhaps you'll be cured of this sort of ailment for the future," they reply.

They exchange knowing glances.

And leave her.

For a while she just lies there, enjoying the sound

of their departing footsteps. And the silence that follows. Then she jumps up.

Suddenly—just as she is standing in the middle of the floor, about to take the bandage off her tummy, and without having heard the sound of footsteps— the door opens.

Oh, good! It's Mandy!

She comes with a tray. She wants to hear, of course, how they're treating her dear Josephine! But Mandy just gives Josephine a long serious look. What could it mean?

If Mandy looks serious, it's for one of two reasons: she's secretly happy about something, or she's sad. Josephine knows this all too well. Impossible to say which it is now! Mandy sets down the tray on the chest-of-drawers. Without a word she fastens the bandage round Josephine's tummy again and adjusts all the others.

"You'd better go back to bed, Miss Josephine," is all she says.

"But Mama thinks . . ."

"Mama doesn't think anything," Mandy interrupts. "She's been in town for three days now and hasn't the remotest idea you're not at school. Come along now, dear, eat up your porridge. It's good for your throat."

"But . . ."

"No buts! The bandage must stay where it is—it'll remind you where you're ill."

And Mandy leaves the room. Her firm steps echo on the stairs.

How *can* she leave Josephine like this? Alone—with all those bandages, and porridge that's getting skin on it? They usually have such lovely times together!

Naturally, it's all Hans' and Gabrielle's fault. They've been telling tales, of course.

As soon as they come home, Josephine's worth no more than the skin on that porridge. It's just to get rid of her—that's something she understands well enough—that they've wrapped her up like this, like a parcel. Just to be able to sit by themselves in peace and quiet, talking grown-up talk.

Well, now they must be pleased with themselves, stupid old gossips!

But Mandy . . . why should she get mixed up in all this?

On the chest-of-drawers stands the porridge bowl. Angrily, Josephine looks at the loathsome stuff. The skin is thick as can be, all wrinkled and nasty. She pulls it off. Then she catches sight of herself in the mirror. What a ridiculous sight! There she stands, with all her bandages and the filthy slimy porridge blanket held up between her fingers.

It's the last straw. Looking at herself in the mirror,

Josephine flings the porridge blanket at it, sticking her tongue out. She sticks her finger in the mess and wipes it about. White lines run down the mirror. It's a nice feeling! It does you good when you're angry!

Then she eats up the porridge—for silly Mandy's sake.

After that she just stands in the window and sulks—a long, long time. Because if you're going to sulk, then you must go on and on with it, so long that everything becomes slightly unreal as if it didn't concern you any more. In the end everything gets so hopeless, it's really lovely.

Grey, hateful, miserable, nasty day!

Now and then a raindrop runs down the window-pane. Outside, the garden lies empty, sad, abandoned. Not a soul in sight. Heavy clouds hang low over the woods.

Sad neighings come floating up from the stable. It's Cockle, the pony. He's standing saddled and ready outside, waiting for Gabrielle. Gabrielle loves to go riding when it rains, but since she also wants to look pretty—when she goes riding, Cockle will have a long wait.

What do I care about good looks? thinks Josephine furiously to herself. Nothing at all! *I* don't want to be kind, or good, or pretty! That's OK for babies, and little sissy girls. Josephine clenches her fists. What she'd most like to do just now is fight.

The trouble with me, she thinks to herself, is I'm wicked, and I like wicked people. Good people bore me. Agreeing with you all the time, when what you want is someone who'll fight back. Just think of that nasty Gunnel . . . Deep down, Josephine really admired her. Gunnel was her Enemy Number One. Scared to death of Gunnel though she was, Josephine shivered with secret delight every time she set eyes on Gunnel. Already Josephine was a lost soul. If she hadn't been so little and weak in those days, she would have fought Gunnel tooth and claw.

Now it's too late. Gunnel had tired of persecuting Josephine long ago. These days she runs after boys who smoke, and smokes herself. She gets cigarettes from her father's sweetshop, and has lots of friends because of them. She doesn't so much as notice a little worm like Josephine any more. Nowadays she has much more interesting enemies. Sadly, Josephine looks out over the garden. I'm no good, she thinks, even as an enemy.

Close at hand she hears the melancholy croaking of a crow. And there he is, floating over the motionless row of trees, down towards the paddock. Calling and calling his lonely cry—and getting no answer.

She gives a sigh of delicious melancholy at all this ugliness, evil, and resentment that are hers. Just imagine—if they only knew what she's really like! Mandy, and Mama, and Papa! But she hides it all away from them. She's false, cunning. *They* think she's good and has the nicest girls in the class for friends. They don't realize she goes her own way— and casts longing glances at the naughtiest little urchins. They haven't the faintest idea of the inky black thoughts inside her head . . .

It's oppressively hot in the room. The tile stove glows and glows.

She throws open the window.

At last, the crow gets his answer. A loud, high-pitched cry is heard from the paddock below. Then all is quiet again. Only the splash of an occasional raindrop and a smell of wet earth and smoke.

The paddock is misty. Down there something black appears. It looks like a great bird, much bigger than the crow.

Again, the cry is heard.

What a strange bird! Dimly, she sees it flapping its wings in the mist. Its cry is so sharp that it seems to linger in the air.

What a strange sound!

And what's that extraordinary creature coming out of the smoke, suddenly becoming visible? Oh no, it's impossible! It's not true!

It can't be . . .

3

Y ES, IT IS! It's Hugo!

With his black mackintosh flapping about him like wings, he comes running at full speed.

And she had hardly dared believe she'd ever see him again!

Hugo is the sort who can vanish at any moment— one must understand that about him. He can come back at any moment, too. Though one never knows exactly when.

No one knows anything about him. And no one asks questions. You wouldn't get an answer if you did. Besides, there's no need to ask. You are happy that he exists. That's enough.

As Josephine stands at her window the garden suddenly becomes transformed before her eyes. It fills with life. Along the washing-line between the cherry tree and a silver birch the raindrops go running, glittering, as if they, too, were alive. In the avenue of limes the leaves sigh and in the grasses are whisperings and patterings of a thousand tiny feet.

As she breathes, faint perfumes come floating up to her, and everywhere she catches glimpses of little birds. They, too, are hiding to witness the miracle down there in the paddock: the great bird that is fluttering towards her.

What a strange day!

Down there Hugo is coming towards her, surrounded by mist. Red leaves are whirling through the air. The crow wheels over his head. The rain drips.

She doesn't feel like fighting any more. No, even though a worthy foe is on the way! Whether Hugo is good or bad, nice or nasty, or even handsome, is something one simply doesn't question.

Hugo is Hugo. And no one else. The rest is unimportant. If anyone knows how to fight back, he does —and everyone knows this.

Deep down inside herself Josephine is laughing. But on the surface she is serious. Should she call him? Or shouldn't she?

No. Don't call. Pretend not to have even seen him. Keep quiet—until he's quite close. Don't say "what a long time it's been!" Try to look as if it were only yesterday. As if she hadn't even noticed that he's been away. Just ask, as usual, whether he'll have lemonade or cocoa . . .

And if he says lemonade, then she'll have cocoa—but if he says cocoa, then she'll have lemonade so as not to show how much she's missed him. Because if she had missed him, she'd want just what he wanted—and so she does. But one mustn't show such things. Not even to oneself.

But why doesn't he come towards the house? Why is he turning off towards the stable? He must have caught sight of Cockle, who stands there stamping, impatient and tired of waiting.

Josephine feels herself pierced by a sharp pang of disappointment. Hugo can never see an animal without putting it before everything else. Look what a hurry he's in now! Running full-tilt.

The next moment Josephine stands paralysed. She hardly understands what has happened, for it all took place so terribly quickly.

Hugo got as far as Cockle, when the pony, grabbing him by his mackintosh, reared violently, shaking his head. Suddenly, against the sky, she sees that great black bird, which a moment ago was running through the paddock, flying high over the stable roof. Now it has vanished.

The horse gives a triumphant neigh.

Then all is quiet. Deathly quiet!

The air stands still. It's as if nothing in the whole world will ever stir again . . .

Except Josephine. Bandages, wrappings, plasters—she doesn't so much as feel them as she rushes out of the room, down the stairs, out of the house, and towards the stable. In her head everything has come to a stop. Only her legs move. And they hardly touch the ground.

By the stable she halts, terrified. Then, pulling herself together, she turns the corner.

What! She can't believe her eyes.

High up on top of the dung heap stands Hugo, so deeply absorbed in some unknown object that he neither hears nor sees anything else. Now he picks it up. It's a beetle. He stuffs it into one of his match-boxes. Then, catching sight of Josephine, he turns pale.

"Josephine! What on earth has happened to you? You're all wrapped up from head to toe."

"It's nothing," she says. He runs down from the top of the dung heap, trips, and falls flat on his face at her feet. Oh, dear! Has he hurt himself? He does look a bit strange, doesn't he?

"You must have concussion," she says. "Lie still, I'll help you."

She tears off her bandages. Hugo lies on his tummy, laughing. She looks at him, anxiously. Of course, he *must* have concussion after such a flight through the air!

She sits down and begins bandaging his head. At first he lets her; then he refuses and shakes his head. He asks if she's out of her wits. But then he lets her go on with it again.

For just a moment he lays his head in her lap. Whether he's a bit weak after his flight through the air, or what, she'll never know—but he lies quite still, staring up at the sky. Suddenly he remarks how blue it is—even though it isn't. Because the rain is still falling. Josephine doesn't reply. (Never contradict people who are injured in the head!) She just band-

ages and bandages, till his whole head is quite soft. Amidst all those bandages his face seems tiny.

"Do you want lemonade or cocoa?" she asks, instead.

"I don't know."

"But . . . tell me."

"You weren't at school today, Josephine?"

"No."

"I was."

"But . . . you've been away for weeks!"

"Have I? As long as that? I was worried when I didn't see you, I thought you might be ill or something."

"Can't you tell me which you want, lemonade or cocoa?"

He gives a little laugh as he looks at her.

"You look just like a mattress, with all those bandages round your tummy. What are they for?"

"Lemonade or cocoa, Hugo?"

"Same as you, then, since you're so stubborn."

She goes all red in the face. Looks away.

"You're impossible," she says.

She starts to walk off. He gets up, and follows her. The bandage on his head wobbles like a huge bird's nest. And his mackintosh flaps.

"Say something," Josephine pleads. "Otherwise I won't know which to have."

"Cocoa, then."

Suddenly she smiles at him, and gives a little skip of sheer happiness.

"Good!" she says, delighted. "Then I'll have lemonade!"

4

SOMETIMES Mandy finds a funny little heap of rubbish on the sitting-room sofa. It might be sawdust, or horsehair, or velvet. Always in the same spot. In one corner. Often a ragged toy animal lies beside it—some poor animal that's lost either its stuffing or its fur.

"Oh!" she says, shaking her head. "Here we go again."

For Mandy knows what it means.

She knows Josephine has been sitting here, so preoccupied that she hasn't noticed how she's been picking the poor little animal to pieces. Mandy knows that Josephine sometimes sits and eavesdrops. But there's nothing she can do about it.

"It's a sin to eavesdrop," she has told Josephine, again and again.

"What would your Mama and Papa say, if they knew?"

Josephine knows. She knows all too well how naughty it is. She knows very well she has sunk to the depths. But she goes on listening, even so. If she didn't, how would she ever get to know anything? It all began when she suddenly realized they were hiding things from her.

She lives in a world of grown-ups. High above her head, the grown-ups' chatter goes on and on. Sometimes their voices are quite open, frank, and ordinary; then she doesn't bother to listen. But when they lower their voices, darkly, then she knows they're full of dangerous secrets.

When everyone falls silent the moment she comes into a room—when they exchange quick hollow looks, laugh high unnatural laughs, begin talking about something else, or suddenly start joking with her—then she knows there's something going on.

No use asking. They just give her hasty, inquiring glances, and say the first thing that comes into their heads. Anything. Without thinking.

They think she doesn't understand when they throw each other meaningful glances and say:

"What big ears you have!"

So she *has* to listen, otherwise she'd worry herself to death. She *has* to know what's threatening her world. That it *is* always being threatened is something she's long understood. Everything will turn out all right in the end, they say—but if so, then why do they whisper so anxiously?

No, they can't fool Josephine! Their lies are white lies, to save her from being frightened; they mean well enough, she understands that. But it only makes her a thousand times more frightened.

But now at long last she's learned what's expected of her. When they play-act, pretending there's nothing dangerous in the whole wide world, then she, too, plays a game of make-believe. But her part is harder to play than theirs, for it's always more difficult to pretend to be deceived than to do the deceiving. And they're all playing the same part; while Josephine, she's all alone in hers.

The evening after Hugo's visit, Josephine sits on the sofa again, in the corner.

In the next room they're talking. The lamps have been lit, and they're drinking tea. The cups tinkle, the radio plays softly.

She longs to go in to them. Outside the windows the night is inky black. There she sits in the dark, her legs getting cold. She has left her slippers upstairs. But not her velvet dog, at which she's anxiously picking, picking, picking. Her fingers move without stopping as she waits and waits . . .

They lowered their voices after dinner today as Hugo's name was mentioned. Once again, she heard that frightening tone of voice. They thought she'd

gone up to the nursery; as soon as they saw her, they began talking in a loud, unnatural way, teasing her. Immediately she felt danger in the air. But she didn't let on.

Now she's sitting here worrying, feeling anxious.

In there are Mama and Hans and Gabrielle. Mama's talking about all she has been doing in town, and then Hans tells her about Cockle. Gabrielle says Cockle didn't mean any harm, tossing Hugo into the air. It was just his little joke. He doesn't know his own strength. It meant he was fond of Hugo—like a friendly thump on the back, so to speak. If he'd been angry, he'd have kicked him.

"But who can ever be angry with Hugo?" Gabrielle says, laughing.

And everyone agrees. Which makes Josephine

[27]

happy. Now she likes them again. They're nice, and mean well. Actually, it was quite funny, all that bandaging and wrapping. And it *had* given her something to wrap Hugo's head in. Otherwise she wouldn't have had anything, would she?

Her courage returns. Maybe she imagined the whole thing? Yes, sometimes she has too much imagination and is altogether too easily scared. Now it sounds quite normal again in there.

Relieved, Josephine gets up to go. But at that moment she hears Mama sigh and say something. So she sinks down again on the sofa.

Oh dear, she just can't hear a thing they're saying! They've turned up the radio now, and are talking quietly. She can hear Hugo's name being mentioned in a strange, solemn fashion. It didn't sound a bit like that, just now. What on earth can it be?

She strains her ears to the utmost, but hears nothing. Only odd words and scraps of sentences.

And now they're talking about something else again. The voices open out and become quite matter-of-fact. Josephine goes up to bed.

But she can't drop off to sleep. For ages and ages she lies there, wide awake, feeling cold. Her feet won't get warm. Was it really just imagination? She doesn't know. And daren't ask. It's so hard, never being able to talk to each other about serious things, only joking all the time. She can talk to Papa-Father, but he never has any time. Nor does Mama. There's always such a lot to be done in churches and vicarages.

She lies thinking about all this, while all through the house the clocks strike in the silent rooms, each in its own corner, each with its own voice, striking and striking, never listening to one another—though they're all clocks, every one of them.

Next morning Mandy finds the little heap of velvet in the sofa. And a poor wretched little dog on the floor. His fur has been plucked away, and he hasn't any ears left.

"Oh, dear me," she says. "So it's like that again, is it?"

Out of troubled eyes she contemplates the little heap of rubbish.

"Now I wonder what the girl's heard now," she thinks to herself. "They ought to have told her immediately. Now there's no guessing how she'll turn and twist it."

5

KARIN IS standing at the school gate, neat and tidy as always. One hand rests on the stone post —so that everyone can see her new light-blue gloves. The boys, of course, just walk past her, hardly throw her a glance.

"Posing for your photo?" asks Edvin, mockingly.

Boys just haven't any taste. But girls have. They all stare and stare at Karin's hands, the envious ones saying nothing, just glowering; the others: "Oh, what lovely gloves! Are they new?"

Josephine hasn't come yet. But now they catch sight of her as she comes along the road. Why can't she hurry up? She drags her feet, keeps turning round. Looking for Hugo, of course.

But he's already at school. Karin has just seen him

—with *green* braces, as always! Yes. And she can't wait to tell Josephine what she thinks about it—what they're *all* thinking. Just as well for her to hear it, because recently she's been leaving Karin in the lurch every day. When Hugo's at school, she spends every minute with him. And if he isn't, then she just keeps to herself, sulking.

Anybody'd think she was in *love* with Hugo. But love's a lot of nonsense—mustn't think such nonsense of one's best friend. Still, it *is* nasty of Josephine. Karin doesn't forget; but Josephine seems to have completely forgotten who her best friend is.

Here she is; but she doesn't so much as notice Karin. She walks backwards, dangling her satchel against her legs. Looks silly, walking like that.

It serves her right that Hugo is at school already. Didn't wait for her. Now maybe she'll understand—and see the difference. Karin justs waits—standing there faithfully at the gate.

But Josephine turns her back on her. She doesn't even turn round as she goes through the gate. Not until Karin calls out:

"Hello, Josephine!"

"Hello—didn't see you . . ."

"No. So I can see! And you don't see anything *else* either."

She spreads her fingers out and waggles them in the blue gloves. Otherwise, she stands stock-still, her plump little body as straight as she possibly can make it, her tummy protruding a bit, and her pigtails sticking out from her head. She gives Josephine a meaningful look and her lips pout, to show how offended she is.

"You must be blind!"

Josephine stares at her, uncomprehending.

"Have you seen Hugo?"

"Of course I have. Long ago."

"Now, I mean. Has he come yet?"

Josephine looks at Karin. Why does she sound so angry? Then Josephine bursts out laughing.

"Why are you standing there with your hand like that, silly? Is it hurting you?"

Karin is dumbfounded. What cheek! She can't find words to express her indignation. Here she has come to school in new gloves, and her best friend has the sauce to ask if she's got a *pain in her hand.* Josephine's even worse than the boys!

Removing her hand from the stone post, Karin places it with dignity on top of her other hand, over her tummy, regarding Josephine with a superior air. But she says nothing.

A couple of girls stop, out of curiosity. Something in the wind here! Might be exciting! More girls turn up. The first ones hide their mouths with the backs of their hands, whispering so loud that everyone can hear:

"Karin and Josephine must be quarrelling . . ."

Puzzled, Josephine stares at them. But now Karin has wind in her sails. *Now* she'll show them.

At that she catches sight of Hugo, across the playground. She bites her lip thoughtfully. She'd really wanted to tell Josephine in *confidence*, what she alone knows—it'd have been so much more well-bred—and Karin has the greatest respect for what is well-bred. But . . .

The temptation is too strong. Her mind made up, she crosses her arms on her chest and throws a disapproving look in Hugo's direction.

"It's a *scandal*," she says.

The others stare. Whatever does she mean?

Scandal—that's a word they've all heard. A word

charged with electricity. Of course, Karin has got it from her mother; that's obvious, because only grown-ups ever dig up scandals. The others stare at her expectantly.

"What is?" asks one.

"Those *green* braces . . ." says Karin.

What about them? Disappointed, they stare at each other. What's so odd about that? Ordinary people don't have green braces perhaps, but Hugo always has. Nothing odd about that, is there? Hasn't she noticed them before?

On the spot they make up their minds to take sides with Josephine—and with Hugo.

"Well, what should he wear, then?" someone asks, pointedly.

"What business is it of yours, anyway?"

"Maybe they ought to be pale blue, eh, like your gloves?"

Hearing that Karin has got new gloves, Josephine comes to her senses. Now she realizes why Karin was so angry with her. From her own experience she knows what it's like, having something new and no one noticing it.

So she says:

"What, have you got new gloves? Oh, how lovely!"

But it's too late. Karin is caught now. She has to keep on. First she lets them babble away; in a moment, when she has said what she's got to say, they'll see how silly they are.

"Or yellow, perhaps, like your pigtails?" titters another.

Karin doesn't reply.

"Your gloves are simply lovely, Karin."

Again, Josephine tries to make herself heard, but the others just throw her scornful looks. Can't she understand they're taking her side? Is she really such a nitwit? Trying to flatter Karin?

But Karin doesn't pay any attention to Josephine. She drops her hands to her sides and says in a serious, reproving voice:

"He ought to be wearing black braces, that's what."

"Well, I don't think so, because black's for funerals."

"You haven't any taste . . ."

"People would think someone's died, that he's in mourning."

Karin stands there motionless, her hands by her sides, and lets them blow off steam. Then she has her moment of triumph.

"That's just what I mean. He *is*!"

Abrupt silence.

Josephine turns icy cold from head to toe. Now she understands why they were talking in such strange solemn voices about Hugo at home! Exactly the sort of voice one uses about someone who's in mourning.

For quite a long while no one says anything. They just stand there staring at each other, completely at a loss, then at Karin, who suddenly looks scared—and ashamed. Already, she regrets not having held her tongue.

"Who is it he's . . .?" someone asks, at last.

"His mother."

Silence again. Karin explains. Her own mother, who works in the telephone exchange, was the first to hear about it. She sounds almost apologetic.

"When was it?"

"A couple of days ago. My mother knew about it at once."

They stand there, bunched closely together, Karin in the middle, Josephine outside, two paces away. They turn their heads, looking timidly about them. No sign of Hugo. They begin whispering . . .

"You can't tell when you look at him."

"No, he doesn't look sad, does he?"

"At least he could wear a black band or something," Karin puts in.

"Maybe he doesn't *want* anyone to know."

"But . . . *green* braces . . ."

"Ssh . . . here comes the teacher . . ."

They look up. Calm, smiling, the teacher comes towards them, waving her arms in the friendliest way, shooing them all in.

"What're you standing here in the middle of the street gossiping for, my little friends? Go on in, get into the playground. The bell will ring any minute now."

They examine her closely. Obviously, she doesn't know anything. Then they look at each other. They'll have to tell her.

"How serious you all look," she says.

Then they tell her, all talking at once. You can see at a glance she didn't know; at first she's dumb-founded. Then the words come tumbling out of her mouth.

"Oh dear, oh dear," she says, "and I was almost angry with Hugo, when he came back!" If she'd only known . . . ! "Poor little fellow, so that's why he's been away so long! And all that talk about spiders . . ."

Suddenly Hugo is there, standing in their midst.

"What's all this whispering about?" he asks calmly.

His green braces gleam brilliantly in the bright sunshine. Everyone gives a jump. They stare at him, as if caught red-handed. Guilty. Ashamed.

On the teacher's forehead a whole spider's web of tiny unhappy wrinkles suddenly appears.

"Hugo," she says, in a low voice. "Forgive me. I hadn't heard . . ."

His gaze gets bluer, deeper, wider than ever. It's as if two wide-awake, penetrating, animal's eyes were looking at her.

"What was it you hadn't heard, Miss?"

"That . . . that your mother . . ."

"Yes. She's dead—but that's my business."

His voice is friendly, but the way he stands and the look in his eyes tells them to mind their own business. Immediately, the little wrinkles vanish from the teacher's forehead.

"I've only just heard about it," she says, hastily. "I want you to know that . . . that we . . . that we feel for . . . and hope . . . and believe . . ."

Suddenly, she falls silent. Hugo makes a little gesture with his hand. A faint smile gleams in his eyes.

"Don't bother trying to cheer me up. It's very kind of you, but there's no need, you see. Because I can do that for myself."

The teacher meets those blue eyes and perhaps wishes she were alone with Hugo just now and could say something quite different. But the others cluster around her like a brood of chicks, seeking her protection. They look timidly at Hugo, realizing how strong and fearless he is.

"I'd cry my eyes out if it were me," whispers one little girl.

"Hugo's mother is all right now," says the teacher, "She's in another and better world . . ."

"What world is that?"

"God's world, child."

A frown appears between Hugo's eyebrows. He puts his thumbs through his braces.

"What about *this* world, then?" he asks. "Who does *it* belong to?"

The teacher blushes slightly and says she meant heaven. Cautiously she asks him if it isn't a happy thought that we go there when we die.

Hugo doesn't reply immediately. The frown is still between his eyes; he looks thoughtful. Then he tips his head backwards and looks up at the sky. Impossible to say whether he's talking to himself or to them:

"I don't know which is nicer," he says. "To think of heaven as something for oneself, that only some people can get into. Or to think of my mother floating about in the sky and feeling at home up there among the sun and the moon and all the other stars. They belong to the same world as ours. Isn't that more probable?"

"But what about the angels, then?" asks Karin. "After all, they've got to live somewhere, haven't they?"

"I don't know anything about them."

"Perhaps you don't believe in angels?"

"Not much."

"Don't you believe your mother's an angel, then?"

Karin feels hurt on Hugo's behalf—and on behalf of all the pretty angels on her bookmarks.

But Hugo sees things quite differently.

"Angel? No, I hope she isn't," he replies, "because she wouldn't like it—it wouldn't suit her, either."

"Surely everyone wants to become an angel," says Karin firmly. And quite a lot of the others agree with her.

But Hugo explains that his mother was the busy sort. She'd never be happy floating about among the clouds and singing or blowing a trumpet. Anyway, she couldn't sing. She preferred the harmonica.

"What she liked best was to go down to the stream and rinse her washing and smoke her pipe. And she believed that's what they'd let her do. And listen to the little birds singing in the woods."

They consider his words. It sounded nice, the way he put it. And yet . . . angel or washerwoman? Most would prefer to be angels.

"Did your mother smoke a pipe?" asks Karin dubiously.

"Sure."

"But you can't do that sort of thing in heaven, can you?" Karin looks serious; she's thinking of the white curtains at home that went all brown from the smoke of her dad's pipe, till her mother got him to stop smoking. She's thinking of the angels' white wings and the clouds. But she doesn't say anything. Suddenly, she's seized by a great feeling of sadness. And uncertainty. And grief. It isn't to her this has happened; she isn't the one who's lost her mother, and yet . . .

She looks across to Josephine, who is standing a

little way away from the others; just like Hugo, but on the other side. Then she sees Josephine's features light up in a way she can't understand. And she feels even more abandoned.

Her eyes dark with fright, she looks back to Hugo.

"It must be terrible, dying," she says in a low voice. And feels frightened by her own words.

The teacher makes a gesture, to show the conversation is over; but Hugo answers in a flash, as he has learned from his father:

"Don't you believe it! I never heard of anyone who didn't manage it all right, though a lot of people can't manage to live . . . That was the bell, Miss . . ."

6

I'LL SOON have to scrape together some money," says Hugo one day, after school. He sounds as if he's looking forward to it, as if it'll be fun.

Josephine looks at him in amazement.

"What, haven't you got any money, either?" she asks.

"You can't have any when you haven't earned any," says Hugo. "But now I'm going to, and that'll be interesting."

She says nothing, just walks quietly along, kicking a stone in front of her.

"I sent my dad away, today," he explains. "He needed a bit of a rest, you see. A change of air. Does everyone good, a change of air."

She nods. She understands, particularly if the air is

full of sadness. Though she doesn't say that. Instead, she asks how long his dad will be away.

"Can't say."

"Who's going to live with you then, while he's away?"

"With me? No one."

He gives her a look, not understanding her.

Perhaps his dad was anxious, didn't like to leave him alone, she explains.

"Nothing to worry about. He knows I'll manage."

"You can come and live with us," says Josephine. She's sure of it; no need to ask them at home.

In no time they're at the vicarage. The sun is shining on the road; the air is quite warm, even though it is late autumn.

Hugo seems to ponder her suggestion. She waits eagerly to hear his reply.

"But what about my animals at home, then? And that heap of wood that has to be chopped by winter?"

"Can't you bring your animals with you?" she suggests.

He shakes his head. Maybe they're not that sort of animals, he says, a little evasively. They wouldn't get on together, his animals and her parents.

"My people are very fond of animals," says Josephine, a bit hurt.

"But you see," says Hugo darkly, "my animals are not so fond of people." He laughs.

"What's the secret, then?" she asks. "Can't you tell me what sort of animals they are?"

"No, I can't, see," he says, as if the very idea were impossible.

He takes a book out of his knapsack.

"I can't tell you until I've looked them up."

"What do you mean? Don't you *know* what sort of animals you've got, then?"

Hugo doesn't reply at once, just turns the leaves of his book.

"I haven't worked out all their species yet, you see. Even in this part of the country there are hundreds of species . . ."

He opens the book at a certain page and points, showing her. A hasty glance over his shoulder is enough for her to see that the pages are full of hundreds of little black insects.

"Spiders," she giggles. Not that she has anything against them, but she can't understand why they're more important than most other things in this world.

Hugo shuts his book and says consolingly, to cheer her up:

"They're not only spiders; there are all kinds of other creatures too."

"I couldn't care less about your insects."

"No, I'm sure you couldn't."

They throw furious glances at each other: Josephine calmly teasing, with raised eyebrows; Hugo indignant, down in the mouth.

"Are you angry, Josephine? It's a waste of time."

She doesn't reply at once. She can't, because she's got the hiccups. She gets them sometimes, when she doesn't know what to do. She hiccups now. Loud and emphatically. Then she finds her tongue.

She asks him how he thinks he's going to manage?

If, first, he's got to earn some money?

And, second, chop up a lot of wood?

And, third, look after hundreds of spiders and other insects?

When does he think he's going to have time to go to school, she asks him.

"Oh, I'll have time for that, too, see . . ." is all the answer she gets.

Then Josephine gives a last hiccup. And not another word does she say.

Hugo and time. According to him, he's got time for everything—but as a matter of fact he hasn't any idea of time at all. The teacher's said that, too.

"Everyone must be punctual," she said once. "And Hugo is no exception."

He answered:

"No, I'm not. But the way people carry on, they're making me be punctual, too, whether I like it or not. People invented time, and it's up to them to see that time does what they want. And not go rushing around after their own invention like a lot of lunatics. Otherwise, how is anyone ever going to get anything done?"

And the teacher had to give in, just as Josephine
does now.

They've arrived at the vicarage. Hugo sits down
on a stone and takes out paper and pen and an old
newspaper.

"I've an idea," he says. "I think we ought to
draw up a kind of financial plan."

"A what?"

"How we're to get some money."

We he said! That's another matter! So she can join
in, too! The financial plan is to be theirs—jointly . . .

And the first suggestion comes from Josephine.

Karin has told her there are empty bottles to be found on the village green. You get fifty öre each for them. Karin doesn't dare go there herself, because her dad's a policeman and wouldn't approve. But Josephine's father is just a clergyman, and he hasn't ever said a word about empty bottles on the village green, one way or the other.

Hugo listens and nods. The plan is approved. At the top of his piece of paper he writes, in capital letters: Plan Number 1: VILLAGE GREEN.

Then he ponders.

"Come on!" cries Josephine eagerly. "Let's have a cup of hot chocolate first. Then we'll go down there." But Hugo tells her one plan isn't enough. You have to have at least three, in case the first one doesn't work. He opens the newspaper and looks at the advertisement page. Josephine sits beside him. Together they read carefully through all the advertisements. Nothing.

"It doesn't matter," he says. "This paper's two years old, at least; it would have been too late anyway."

"What're we reading it for, then?" asks Josephine.

She looks at him indignantly—such a lot of her time, all wasted!

"I just thought we'd see how those business people fix up things for themselves," he explains. "But there wasn't much to learn."

"Wait a minute!" Josephine runs into the house to get today's paper.

But it's just as bad. Nothing at all in their line.

Suddenly Hugo's gaze settles on the back page. Instantly, he's excited.

"Josephine, look here!"

Yes, she can see. She has no idea what it means.

"HAVE YOU THE WRITING ITCH?" are the words written in huge letters.

And beneath: *Ring or write to us.*

"The writing itch? What's that?" she asks impatiently.

"I don't know. Go on reading!"

She reads and reads, the words spin round and round in her head, and she can't make any sense of them at all. But Hugo looks as if someone had sent him a birthday present.

"Isn't it exciting?"

How stupid she feels. She gives him an uncomprehending stare. What's so exciting about such drivel?

"It says you can write at home. Anything. And they pay for it."

"Oh?" She thinks the matter over.

"But you've got to have the writing itch," she says, doubtfully. "And you don't know what that is."

"Itch—that's when it itches. It must mean some people itch when they write."

Yes, that must be it! Josephine has heard of people

like that. Mandy knows an old woman whose hands itch dreadfully whenever she knits with a particular type of wool. And another old woman has an itch in her arms when she does the washing. Mandy often talks about it.

"Then they must have made a stupid mistake," says Hugo. "Of course, it means if you *haven't* got the writing itch, you're to let them know."

"Of course. They've left out a word."

"It's easily done," says Hugo magnanimously, and writes in big letters: Plan Number 2: WRITING ITCH.

"But what will you write about?" asks Josephine.

"We'll see about that later; I'll think up something . . ."

He looks cunning. A suspicion enters her mind.

"Not about spiders," she says seriously. "There are people who're scared of spiders."

He tells her not to worry. He knows that.

"People don't realize spiders were here on earth long before themselves," he says gloomily.

Then he writes in big letters: Plan Number 3: THE MAIL.

They run in and drink up their hot chocolate in a great hurry.

No good ringing up the paper; someone might hear. So Hugo sits down and writes. With a serious expression on his face, he writes the following letter:

WRITING ITCH IS SOMETHING I HAVEN'T GOT. BECAUSE THEN I WOULDN'T WRITE. BY THE WAY YOU'VE LEFT OUT A WORD IN YOUR ADVERTISE-MENT.

NO ONE'S EVER WRITTEN FROM THIS VILLAGE YET. A PITY. I'LL DO IT NOW.

I WON'T WRITE A WORD ABOUT SPIDERS EVEN THOUGH THERE ARE DOZENS OF SPECIES IN ONE LITTLE TINY SPOT IN THIS VILLAGE. I KNOW WHAT VIEWS PEOPLE HAVE CONCERNING THESE ANI-MALS.

PEOPLE ARE RARER, BUT THERE ARE ENOUGH. NOT MANY ARE AS INTEREST-ING AS SPIDERS, HOWEVER, BUT THEY WANT TO GET THEIR NAMES AND PIC-TURES IN THE PAPER. THEY LIVE ON THE LAND OR IN THE WOODS.

THE MEN DON'T SAY MUCH. THE WOM-EN TALK. THE CHILDREN JUST STARE. EVERYBODY HAS A LONG LIFE. IF SOME-ONE DIES TOO EARLY IT'S BECAUSE SHE'S WANTED SOMEWHERE ELSE.

WHEN I'M READY I'LL WRITE AGAIN.
                                   KIND REGARDS,
                                   HUGO ANDERSSON

Silent, respectful, Josephine reads the letter. Hugo spells like a book—not at all as he speaks.

"Yes," he says. "You have to know how to spell properly, otherwise you couldn't read or write."

7

I T ' S QUITE a distance to the village. When you hear the shots coming from it on Sunday mornings, you wouldn't think it lay so far away. Or the music on Saturday evenings. Then it seems quite close. But it's a long way to push a wheelbarrow.

First you go quite a long way along the road; then you turn off into the woods. Here you can see it's autumn; the path is thick with yellow leaves and the ferns have turned red. If you bend down you can smell mushrooms and damp earth; if you hold your nose up, there's a smell of sunshine. And your nose tickles.

When Hugo and Josephine reach the stream they stop. It is broad, but so shallow you can reach the pebbles on its bottom. The water glitters and the stones are ice-cold; it takes a long time before they warm up in your hand.

Josephine holds them up high, as close to the sun as possible. Then she sniffs at them.

"They smell of the Stone Age," she says.

And she thinks for a while of the Stone Age, when the children were all perfectly free and the pigs were wild and ran about in the woods all day, and the sun shone and everywhere were trickling streams like this one.

"The black ones are flint," says Hugo sniffing at the pebbles like a beast of prey at its victim. "The others I have to find out about."

But Josephine is still in the Stone Age.

"Flint," she repeats, looking dreamily at the stone.

"There's grey flint, too, and speckled . . ."

The sunshine floods down on the pebble in her hand.

"Same sun then," she says.

"Very dense sort of stone, this."

"And the same stones . . ."

"But easy to split, see. That's why they used them in the Stone Age."

Suddenly Josephine looks at Hugo, as if she saw him for the very first time.

"Only you and I are new here," she says.

He reflects on her words, then says:

"Well, we're not so new, either. Humanity's older than . . ."

"*Humanity*," she interrupts. "But I'm talking about you and me."

"Really? And that's something else, is it?"

He picks up the wheelbarrow and holds it carefully as he steps across the stones in the stream.

Josephine follows him.

The green is deserted now. The last Saturday-night dance was held several weeks ago, although the rifle range is still in use.

They begin poking about in the bushes and undergrowth where you usually find old bottles, but today they can't find a single one.

"Odd. Karin said there were heaps of them."

"Maybe they've already been here and taken them."

Josephine is ashamed. It was her plan—and she's made a mess of it. Pushing the wheelbarrow all this way for nothing!

But Hugo doesn't worry. He's in the woods now, and that's never a waste of time.

You never know what he'll be up to next. One moment he's up in a tree, the next lying in some hole. Suddenly you can't see him at all—he can vanish like an animal, without a sound. Again and again you have to call to him. Sometimes his answer comes from high up, sometimes from beneath your feet.

Just now he's lying flat on the ground. Josephine stares at him listlessly. Then he holds out his hand.

Something glitters in it. Without a word he jumps up and pours into her hand a stream of tiny glittering balls.

They're the tiniest little things, the sort people want most of all. People do anything to get hold of such things. She only owns one single ball, much bigger than these, and not at all shiny—a bit rusty, in fact; that's why she was able to swap something for it. These are small but heavy for their size and gleam as if they were pure silver.

"They use them inside cartridges to shoot with." His voice is quite calm but has an undertone of excitement.

"Did you find them *there*?"

"Yes. There are heaps and heaps of them. You've only got to look for them."

Then he throws himself down on the ground again, and Josephine does, too.

You can't see the little balls when you're standing up; you have to creep about on all fours to find them. They hide under leaves, in the grass, in the moss, everywhere. Some have bored their way into the ground—just scratch a little and your hand's full of them.

Some are rusty. They've lain there too long. But most are lovely and shiny.

"Once I dreamed I found a heap of coins in a ditch," Josephine tells him. "I dug and dug, and found more and more. It was horrible waking up. I suppose this is only a dream, too."

"This isn't—this is reality." He throws her a swift convincing glance. His eyes are blue as blue. Then in a flash he has vanished again, but suddenly reappears behind an old target.

"Over here they usually shoot with an air gun," he says.

And he hands her a little arrow with a soft red tuft.

Then Josephine finds seven of them, and Hugo eighteen. The tufts are of different colours, blue, yellow, red—all as bright as can be.

They stand facing each other, feeling a bit giddy.

"We're happy," she says, "and rich!"

She sticks her nose into the tufts, which tickle so that you squeak with laughter. She sticks her hand in her pocket and digs her fingers among all the little balls, letting them trickle between her fingers. They feel cool and rattle and tinkle. She wallows in a greedy feeling of how rich she is.

"This is better than bottles," says Hugo. "How much can we get for each of them, do you think? Five öre apiece? Or three for five öre?"

"Are you going to sell yours?"

"Of course! Have you forgotten we're trying to earn money?"

Yes, she had. She looks confused.

"I'm never going to sell *mine*," she says, indignantly. "Never as long as I live. When for once I've found a treasure . . ."

"Do what you like; no one's forcing you. But I've got to. And there'll be more pellets here every time they do some shooting."

Josephine jumps back on to the path. Hugo pushes the wheelbarrow, while she just talks and talks. They mustn't tell anyone about this. Not a word. Or their tongues'll turn black.

"No. This isn't anyone else's business," he says.

"But supposing they ask us where we got all the pellets?"

"Then we'll tell them to mind their own business."

"Won't they get angry?"

"They'd better not . . ."

He sounds quietly determined. She goes on chattering happily. Who'd have thought such a thing could happen on an ordinary day like this? In the morning you go to school, as usual, have to wear woollen socks that tickle—and think to yourself "This is going to be a horrible, nasty day"—and then suddenly everything changes. What day is it? Tuesday . . . Then Tuesday's going to be her lucky day. What date? The twelfth . . . Twelve's her lucky number.

Hugo replies from time to time, but his glance wanders. Suddenly he has vanished again. The wheelbarrow is left standing on the path.

A moment later he calls:

"Josephine! Can you come over here?"

His head pops up behind a stone. She runs over.

The whole ground is covered with mushrooms, yellow and gleaming in the sunshine. Again, she throws herself down on the ground and silently starts picking. The two of them are speechless at such a sight. They fill the wheelbarrow. Carefully, they push it in front of them; it looks as if it were full of gold bars. Silent, they walk through the wood.

On reaching the road Josephine suddenly comes to a halt, and asks:

"What was that man called who discovered America?"

"Columbus."

She nods. And smiles with pleasure at her own thoughts: when things like this happen, it's almost as if you were someone else, hardly an ordinary person at all, as if . . .

"You turn into Columbus . . ." she says in a dreamy voice.

Hugo looks at her.

"I hope all those riches haven't gone to your head?" he asks.

At that moment someone appears in front of them on the road. Someone Josephine seems to have seen before, somewhere. An old woman on a bicycle. Yes, someone she knows all too well.

Her heart flies up into her throat.

In a flash she's swept back—not merely to reality but to another time. A horrid, childish time, long before she met Hugo. When she understood nothing. She isn't Columbus any more, she's . . .

"Josephine, my little pet? What, don't ye know Granny Lyra?"

Her knees trembling, Josephine nods. She feels as if she could sink into the earth.

The old woman gets off her bicycle and embraces her. Josephine twists and squirms. If she could, she'd

run for her life, but she just stands there paralysed.

There was a time when she used to run and see this old woman every day. Granny Lyra she called her, because she always wanted a Granny of her own and didn't have one. At that time she thought Granny Lyra was the nicest person in the whole wide world.

But she wasn't. Josephine found that out. And it wasn't a pleasant discovery. Since then she hadn't wanted to talk to Granny Lyra any more. And so far she hasn't had to. She's always caught sight of her in time and beaten it as fast as one could go.

Why not today? Her lucky day?

How strange everything is! Upside-down. Is it always like this? Of course, you don't notice it on ordinary days—days when there's not much difference anyway, which way things are. But a day like *this* one—when everything had been the right way up, then they obviously have to turn upside-down, too.

The old woman talks and talks like a downpour; she stands there and says what a *terribly* long time it has been since she's seen Josephine.

"Why haven't you been to see me, my pet? Have you forgotten poor Granny Lyra who gave you all those lollipops?"

Josephine can't get a word out. The sun is setting, the shadows become long and pointed, it's getting cold. She shivers and her teeth chatter, as the old woman says:

"Poor little thing, and such thin clothes, always!"

Now Hugo announces his presence. He had gone along ahead with the wheelbarrow and hadn't noticed that Josephine had stopped. But now he appears on the scene and interrupts Granny Lyra in the midst of her stream of lamentations.

"How about some mushrooms? We just picked them," he says. "Dry as can be, though it's so late in the autumn."

Granny Lyra's glance flits over him and her nasty little bad-tempered eyes light up like black pills. She breathes deeply, curious and greedy, as if she'd just discovered something. As she turns to Josephine and points to Hugo, she makes a whistling sound through her nose.

"Are you keeping company with that young scamp?" she asks.

It is Hugo who answers:

"Terrible loud whistling sound coming out of your nose! You'd better go to the doctor."

Panic-stricken, Granny Lyra seizes her nose.

"It's only when I get excited," she says.

Hugo nods and looks as if he were a specialist on squeaky noses.

"Better take care not to get excited, then," he says blandly. "But how about the mushrooms? They're certainly the last ones this year."

"How much do they cost?"

"Twenty-five öre a pint. They were asking fifty in

the market in town a month ago, so they're cheap."

The old woman picks up a mushroom and pinches it—suspiciously, as if she were squeezing a dead rat.

"Has Josephine been picking these, too?" she asks. "You mean to say the minister's daughter's been . . ."

Her nose gives a loud squeak. Abruptly, she falls silent. Hugo fixes his stare on it, lets it rest there. His expression is one of worried sympathy; his eyebrows move, but he says nothing.

Nervously, Granny Lyra squeezes the mushrooms, breaks them, one after the other, examines them nearsightedly.

"No worms in them," Hugo informs her.

The old woman gives him a sharp look.

"Three pints," she says at last, holding out her basket, which has been hanging from her bike, "I'll just take three pints."

Hugo fills it to the brim. Granny Lyra searches in her purse and takes out three twenty-five öre pieces. But she stands holding the coins, and she looks craftily from one to the other.

"Who's to have the money, then?" she asks, ingratiatingly. "Maybe you want to share it? Because Josephine, after all . . ."

Another squeak from her nose.

Josephine makes no move, but Hugo puts out his hand; and the old woman, disgruntled, gives him the money.

"Thanks," he says politely. "But you'd better take care of that nose of yours, that's my advice. Don't go sticking it into places where it doesn't belong, because it won't stand much of that sort of thing. 'Bye."

Suddenly Granny Lyra tries to find her tongue again; words pile up on it, jostling to get out, and her nose squeaks and squeaks. And so loud! But not a word comes out. She just stands there gaping. Then, with surprising agility for one of her advanced age, she hops on her bicycle, and whirls away like a dervish. She doesn't even say good-bye to Josephine.

Hugo stands looking after her with a strange mixture of expressions on his face. Sly and satisfied—but at the same time a bit ashamed. And there is a grim sound in his voice, as he says:

"You shouldn't talk like that to such an old person, really you shouldn't. Just now I'm not pleased with myself."

Josephine doesn't reply. The whole meeting has shaken her. Of course, it had to happen some time. And it was a good thing Hugo was there. Maybe he wasn't as polite to Granny Lyra as he ought to have been, but she deserved no better. And Josephine feels strangely relieved. As if someone who had long been persecuting her had gone up in smoke.

Neither says anything for a while, then Hugo lets the whole thing blow over. He gives a wry smile.

"It's a long time until Easter," he says, "but that

8

THEY GOT five kroner twenty öre for their mushrooms. Hugo wants to go halves with Josephine. But she shakes her head.

"It was you who found the mushrooms."

She explains: The money would take all the fun out of the pellets. It'd be too much—too much luck for one day. For him it's different, since he isn't going to keep his pellets. She gives him an appealing look. Can't he understand?

He has his doubts, but he understands.

"I'll give you something one day, Josephine. I'll think up something special, something for you."

He looks up at the top of the trees, and his voice sounds a shade more formal and ceremonious than usual; it's a solemn promise he's making. She understands that. Although she doesn't say anything, she's happy—so happy she can't answer a word.

"That's something I must think over properly," he says.

She nods and finds she's in a hurry to get home. He, too, for he has a long way to go.

The next day is a veritable market day in the school playground. They have no difficulty in selling the pellets. Everybody struggles to get some, not only their own class, but the whole school. No one bothers to ask where they came from. Everyone is used to Hugo doing things no one else can.

The little balls soon come to an end, and Hugo and Josephine hurry off after school to the green to fetch some more. And so it goes on, for several days. Hugo can't collect pellets too quickly.

But one fine day their secret is betrayed. No one has been gossiping. It's just that the father of one girl goes shooting down at the green, and of course he has no difficulty in working out where all the pellets are coming from. It's heart-breaking, but what can they do? That day the green is full of children searching for pellets. Not that they find very many. For one thing, they haven't Hugo's financial urge, and anyway the pellets are beginning to come to an end.

So that's the end of the first "financial plan". And now winter's at the door. That will make everything more difficult.

Next day there is a big notice stuck up on the door of the Post Office:

TAKE YOUR MAIL HOME FOR YOU
DAILY
APPLY TO
HUGO ANDERSSON
CHARGE 25 ORE

When school is over, Hugo goes down to the Post Office and asks:

"Anyone been making any applications yet?"

And on the very first day he gets two customers. The news spreads. Now, with the autumn rains coming on, many feel relieved not to have to go to the post every day. But they don't want to miss their mail and their newspaper.

In the end he has so many people to fetch mail for, he hardly has time for them all. They live far apart, and he hasn't a bike. Sometimes Josephine lends a hand, and they take the wheelbarrow, in order to be able to carry it all at once. Even so it takes time.

"I ought to have a bike," says Hugo, "then it would be done quick as a wink."

Josephine hasn't got one either and won't until she's twelve. And that's several years away. But suddenly she remembers—of course! There's an old bicycle at home in the vicarage!

"It's as old as the hills, though," she says. "At least a hundred years old and looks dreadful."

"Where have they got it?"

"In the old coach-house."

"Let's go and see."

Even the key to the carriage house is awful: huge, heavy, and rusty. Josephine stands awhile, plucking up courage; then she hands it to Hugo.

"You unlock it."

The door creaks and squeaks ominously. There's not even a threshold. One feels as if one were being sucked inside. Nasty sort of a place, it is, with an old musty smell. It makes one shiver and one's teeth chatter.

Yes, the coach-house is ghostly. Hardly anyone ever comes in here. But when they do, Josephine, frightened though she is, always comes with them. Something attracts her to it, against her will. It's odd.

After the squeak of the door—silence. A terrifying silence—as if all noises had suddenly died. Inside, only a chilly desolation and stillness reign, as if all objects had gone to sleep and stiffened forever.

A black-covered carriage stands in front; one of its wheels is loose and bent, a window has been smashed, the footplate is rusty and worn. The whole carriage looks as if it had jumped straight out of a ghost story. Further inside, one can glimpse a ramshackle haywagon and an old sledge; everywhere there lie broken wheels, shattered barrels, boxes, benches, and all sorts of junk, all covered in a thick layer of dust, with every hole and corner thick with spiders' webs.

"Pretty," says Hugo. "Very nice."

Josephine doesn't see anything pretty about it, but her glance falls on a pair of shiny rat's eyes which peer out from the carriage window and then, a minute later, without the faintest rustle, vanish. A ghost rat?

Suddenly, a clock starts ticking. It comes from the depths of the silence: tick-tock-tick-tock. As clear as can be. Just a short while. Then silence again.

"Hear that?"

Hugo nods, his eyes shining.

Then the ticking begins again, louder now. Josephine goes all cold and stiff. A clock. But where? And whose?

Either it's a ghost clock, starting and stopping of its own accord, or else there's someone in here, hiding, who has a watch. Someone who is trying to stop it ticking, so that it shan't betray his whereabouts.

The one idea seems as monstrous as the other. In a voice half-strangled by horror, she whispers:

"Hugo, let's get out of here!"

The clock ticks louder and louder. Sometimes it stops. Then goes on ticking again.

Suddenly Josephine catches sight of the door, which throws an enormous shadow on the ground outside. The shadow quivers. All at once the door slams shut with a crash. In the shed it's as black as night. She gives a scream.

"What are you screaming for?"

"Someone's slammed the door! We're shut in!"

Hugo throws her an eloquent glance.

"Maybe you haven't noticed how hard the wind's blowing today?"

He goes and pushes open the door.

"Just blew shut, that's all."

"But . . . what about that clock? It's ticking . . ."

"Yes. It's a deathwatch."

Her eyes almost start out of her head. She thinks she's going to faint. A ghost watch!

Hugo pokes about in the shed. What, is he actually *looking for it*? How dare he? Putting his ear against an old wooden chest, he listens.

"Must be in here," he says.

He opens the lid.

"Here," he says. "Come and have a look."

She creeps over, but sees nothing. The chest is as empty as can be. He points at some little holes in the lid and mysterious little heaps of what seem to be flour, which lie all over its bottom.

"These are traces of a deathwatch," says he.

The ticking has stopped altogether. Did the ghost clock turn into dust when he discovered it?

"No. A deathwatch is a little beetle who likes to gnaw at old wood. They snap their jaws together when they call to each other. And it sounds just like a clock ticking."

She gives him a sceptical look. Now he *must* be imagining things! He thinks everything in the world comes from spiders and beetles.

"I'm not fooling," he says. "It's the truth. People call them deathwatches but it's just a lot of old super-stition."

She only half believes him. But her fright is gone.

"Shall we get the bike out now?" she asks, and begins moving towards a steep ladder that leads up to the loft.

It's dark up there. The window is small and cov-ered with spiders' webs In one corner hangs a huge deserted wasps' nest.

It's quite a while before they find the bicycle—if it really is a bicycle. When she sees it, Josephine scarcely believes it can be.

"It belonged to my great-grandfather when he was little," she says apologetically. "It can't be ridden now, I don't think."

"Certainly isn't an ordinary one," declares Hugo, who seems as pleased as can be. He finds a rag and wipes off the dust. A mysterious sea-green colour be-gins to appear. It's lovely! The front wheel is much bigger than the back wheel, and has the pedals on it—instead of between the wheels, as they are on or-dinary bicycles. It's quite a hard job getting it down the ladder, but Hugo is strong and obstinate. Josephine follows behind, holding tight so that the monster won't fall on him. It does, even so; but luckily they are almost at the bottom by now, and there's more noise than damage.

The bicycle squeaks loudly as they push it out into the yard. But it can be oiled.

"She's rolling, and that's the main thing," says Hugo.

He pushes it over to the fence. To get up on its saddle he'll have to climb up on to something high. In the end, one way or another, he succeeds in this piece of acrobatics. It looks as if he's taking his life in his hands, and the machine squeaks deafeningly. But he cycles for several yards before he comes tumbling off.

"Heavens! Have you hurt yourself?"

He shakes his head. Nothing can stop him now. Josephine runs for some oil and tools. Feverishly he starts repairing it.

After a couple of hours the bike is ready.

"It's a monster," he says proudly. "It'll be like a circus act, when I come riding by."

"But you'll never learn to ride that thing," says Josephine dubiously.

"Won't I? People have ridden it before, haven't they? Then I can ride it now."

"But that was ages and ages ago."

"Do you think it was easier then? Or do you think they were built differently from us?"

He falls off again and again. But he doesn't give up. Again and again he lies there on the ground with the monster on top of him, all tangled up in its front wheel. He gets scratches on his arms and knees.

"That's *nothing* to fuss about," he says when Josephine points them out to him.

The cycle is running quietly now. All the noise is gone. By and by he learns to control it.

"It's a fine bike, strong and durable," he says.

But he has to watch out for cart tracks and stones. On the road it goes better.

It's not long before Hugo is sitting as firm in the

saddle as he would on any other bicycle. And every day he can be seen riding "the monster", as he takes people their mail. At first the sight attracts a certain amount of attention, though no one says anything. If it's Hugo, everything's all right. The most ridiculous things seem perfectly natural.

Except to Karin, poor wretch, who's a bit jealous. She whispers that her dad, the policeman, could arrest Hugo, if he wanted to. Because Hugo's a *traffic menace*. But no one cares.

On the contrary—everyone feels very grey, ordinary, dull, and down-to-earth, as they cycle along on their ordinary bikes. Everyone is secretly dreaming of having a bicycle like Hugo's. He floats along the road—head and shoulders above everyone else. High up. Alone. Free.

9

"NOW SHE'S COME."

Karin comes running, her heart in her throat.

"She's standing talking to your teacher in the corridor. Her mother's there, too."

Josephine knows who Karin means. The last few days they've been talking about nothing but the new girl. But Josephine has had other things to think about.

"Lucky thing! Of course she would have to go and join *your* class."

Josephine doesn't feel particularly lucky—or even curious. She feels nothing at all. Sometimes one doesn't.

"Her mother seems wonderful. She said good morning to me."

Karin goes on talking. Josephine doesn't answer.

She wonders why she suddenly feels as though thorns were growing on her soul.

Right in the middle of the village, not far from the shop, stands a big white house, in a lovely old garden. An old woman lives alone in it with her dog. The dog is as tall as a calf and spotted as a leopard, but perfectly friendly. The lady is rather old. She is the new girl's grandmother. They're to live with her now, the girl and her mother.

Her dad's dead. Drowned last summer, Karin tells Josephine. That's why they've moved here.

"They're as rich as can be, so I've heard. Her mother's got a *huge* car."

They're standing behind the school-house, waiting for the bell to ring. As Karin goes on talking, Josephine looks at her expectantly, but can't find anything to say. She has a feeling of being empty, a bit spiteful and full of vague, nasty premonitions—all at the same time. Karin's delight at the new girl and her mother irritates her. What on earth has the girl to do with them?

Josephine's glance settles on the notice on the door to the boiler-house. She has seen it every day of her life, but not until this moment has she discovered it. It says: UNAUTHORIZED PERSONS NOT ADMITTED. For a long while she stares at the words.

Then the bell rings. And as they run round the

corner, the new girl and her mother come out of the front door. They come face to face. Karin stops and smiles, the mother smiles and nods.

But Josephine stares at the girl. She sees long black hair, which shines and gleams and curls at the ends, a broad wide forehead with dark eyes looking straight ahead, and a little mouth that looks as if it hadn't much to say.

Josephine looks at the new girl, but she doesn't look at Josephine. She goes on walking seriously beside her smiling mother.

Without knowing why, Josephine finds she is thinking about the notice she was staring at just now —the words on the door to the boiler-house. She drives away the thought.

"What's her name?" Josephine asks.

"I don't know," Karin replies.

They follow her with their eyes. She walks straight-backed, without looking either to the right or the left. Karin looks a trifle thoughtful.

"Of course, she might just be a conceited little ninny," she says. "But her mother's wonderful."

Josephine doesn't reply. She wonders whether she likes the new girl, and then wonders why she's wondering . . .

After the day's last lesson the teacher says tomorrow they're going to have a new classmate, called

Miriam. Josephine throws a look at Hugo, who doesn't look back.

Oh—so it's Miriam . . .

Next day there's an empty desk in front of Hugo's.

That's where she's to sit. But she hasn't turned up.

They have drawing. The teacher has drawn a tree on the blackboard, which they're to copy. They all get busy—except Hugo. He just scratches his neck and stares at the blackboard.

"I can't see what sort of tree it is," he says. "What's it supposed to be? An oak or an ash or what?"

"Just draw that tree, Hugo. It doesn't make any difference what it is."

Hugo considers whether he'll do what the teacher tells him, but his conscience seems to prevent him.

"Of course it does," he says. "Of course, it makes a difference." And he begins drawing the Philippine national flag instead.

At that moment there's a knock at the door and the teacher goes over and opens it.

It's Miriam.

Everyone stops drawing and looks up. They stare so hard that Josephine is positively embarrassed. She crouches over her tree and rubs it with her india rubber. That's what they always do when someone comes into the classroom—stare. But this time there's something special about it. Their eyes pierce Miriam like arrows. Just because there has been such a lot of talk about her before. Only Hugo doesn't look up, not even once. He's only interested in his flag.

Her back almost unnaturally straight, Miriam stands in front of the teacher. The teacher, a bit embarrassed by all the stares, tells her she is welcome. She drops her handkerchief. Miriam picks it up.

"Where am I to sit?" she asks, and the teacher points to the desk in front of Hugo. Without a glance at anyone, she goes over and sits down quickly, takes out her pencils and paper and begins drawing the tree.

Everyone goes on staring, but all they can see is a bent back in a black-and-white checked dress and dark hair. They're disappointed. Nothing more is to be got out of the new girl's arrival in the class.

A faint smell of soap—or can it be scent—reaches Josephine. She looks up timidly. Just for one moment Miriam turns her profile towards her, looking out of the window. Her nose is a little curved; proud, superior, it stands out against the blackboard. She runs her hand through her hair. It could really be a boy's hand, large and blunt, with nails bitten ragged. It is not proud and scornful like her profile.

Josephine looks at her own hand—it's thin. As for her profile, there's nothing superior about it, she knows that. Miriam is beautiful. Josephine isn't. Again she looks at Hugo, but he doesn't once look up.

After the lesson, as they're going out, Miriam is suddenly standing beside Hugo's desk, and Josephine hears her say:

"Thanks for not staring at me like a lunatic."

Hugo slams down his desk-top and looks at her.

"Stare? What for? I don't see any reason to stare."

His eyes are blue as blue.

"No," says Miriam. "Nor do I." Then she runs off.

And Hugo disappears behind the top of his desk again. Josephine doesn't wait for him.

At break all the girls gather round Miriam. Except Josephine. She watches it all at a distance. Miriam isn't just the *new* girl, she's the *pretty*, the *smart*, the *rich* girl. She's a queen. Everyone wants to belong to her court. To be her best friend perhaps . . .

But it's not long before Josephine notices that the crowd around Miriam isn't as thick as it was before. One by one they leave her. Soon she's standing there just as much alone as Josephine. She doesn't want a court; she doesn't need one. Now she walks quickly across the playground, her back as straight as a ramrod, without ever looking about her.

The same thing happens every break, and every lesson. Miriam sits bolt upright, still as can be, staring straight in front of her answering questions in her clear but low voice, answering exactly as she should, with not a word more. It's impossible to get to know her.

Soon it doesn't occur to anyone to try. She's stuck-up, they say, just because she's rich; she thinks she's pretty, that she's superior.

"I was right," says Karin. "She's conceited. But her mother's wonderful."

Josephine thinks the whole thing is incomprehensible. Everything that at first was regarded as remarkable about Miriam is transformed overnight into a drawback. Why?

For her part she feels somehow shy and timid.

Miriam doesn't make any fuss about herself. And she's impossible to approach. Her presence—from that day on—makes itself felt more than anyone else's, except perhaps Hugo's. But that is another matter.

10

ONE DAY there's a storm blowing. Hugo and Josephine are on their way home.

If you walk straight into the wind, you can hardly breathe. You choke. And you have to yell to talk. The wind grabs at your words as they come off your tongue. You can't even hear yourself.

That's why they're walking backwards—and don't see the car. The brakes squeal and howl behind their backs, but they think it's just the gale. Suddenly, they hit something hard, and Josephine's lying at the edge of the road. Luckily, the car had already come to a dead stop, so she isn't hurt; she just lost her balance from sheer terror.

"That was a near thing! I almost ran over you," she can hear a frightened voice saying.

It is Miriam's mother.

"It's blowing," Hugo remarks by way of excuse.

"So I see," she says. And then asks if they wouldn't like to come home with her in the car and have some lemonade.

"Miriam would be so happy," she says. "She still doesn't know any of you and hasn't anyone to play with."

Josephine wonders whether Miriam would really be so happy. But they accept her offer. Particularly as they'll get a ride home afterwards.

The huge dog is lying on the front steps, but he doesn't stir as they approach. He just wags his tail a little and puts his tongue out. Miriam's granny comes out to meet them. She greets them with a friendly but distracted smile. It is the same smile that she gives when you meet her on the road with her dog: a smile that means nothing, as if she didn't know at whom she was smiling—or care. Perhaps she doesn't even know she *is* smiling. She seems very absent-minded. Now she invites them in.

The rooms in her house are as big as oceans. Her furniture is tall, heavy, and dark. Among its massiveness she seems a lost shadow that could evaporate at any moment. She seems as light and frail and trans-parent as air. As she goes ahead to draw aside a heavy curtain, there is a pause. The curtain sweeps back—as if to wipe her out. But she escapes. Smiling, she is already standing in the next room under a gigantic chandelier. Josephine looks at her anxiously. Anyone as frail and fragile as that must find every minute dangerous in a house that's so much too big for her.

"I suppose Miriam's in her room?" asks her mother. She goes to fetch her.

They're standing in the library. Its walls are covered with bookcases. Hugo stops in front of them and begins behaving mysteriously. There he stands, sniffing and nosing about, like a hunting dog on the scent.

"This has a most unusual characteristic smell," he says.

"We did dust in here only last week," replies the grandmother, with a faint smile.

"Luckily, it didn't help. Old books always smell, anyhow."

The grandmother gives him a confused look.

"Are you interested in books, Hugo?" she asks.

"Yes," says Hugo, "because there's a lot hidden away in them. Particularly if they're old. There isn't much in the new ones."

The old lady's eyes light up. Her vague look vanishes. She seems almost lively.

"What you say is so true!" she exclaims. "I can't find anything in modern literature, either."

"But there are people who can't find anything in old books as well. They just let their eyes wander over the letters and don't see anything."

Miriam's grandmother becomes livelier and livelier. Colour has come into her cheeks, and she nods emphatically at Hugo's words of wisdom.

"Quite right," she says, "people have no eye for what really matters, but in a lot of books that really isn't easy to find either; one has to learn how to search for the soul of a book . . ."

"That's a good name for it, the soul of a book, that's just what you might call it . . . I'll remember that . . ."

Hugo is very talkative; he loves to get involved in a discussion. The grandmother clasps her thin white hands enthusiastically.

"It's so strange," she says. "Sometimes you think you can see quite clearly, you think you've really found a book's soul . . . And then suddenly—it's vanished."

"That's because it can run backwards and forwards."

At that moment Miriam comes in. With a serious expression, she shakes hands, first with Josephine, then with Hugo.

"Nice to see you," she says politely. And not a word more.

Light as a lark the grandmother trips over to her daughter and says in a low voice, delightedly:

"This little fellow's got the right ideas about books. You can talk to him like an adult. He's a real bookworm."

"How nice," says Miriam's mother, then looks to

see where Miriam is. She's standing looking out of the window.

Hugo has taken a thick book down from the shelf and is turning the pages with the ease of someone who is always looking through books.

"You always think you'll find something in the thickest volumes," he says. "But that's a mistake, you can be sure."

The grandmother exchanges a delighted and knowing glance with Miriam's mother and says she agrees: there's not much to be found in those old French novels.

"So I see," says Hugo, and puts the volume back.

Josephine feels like a perfect nitwit. Hugo's interest in books is something rather new to her. They have lots of books at home, but she has paid them little attention. She remembers how once he had let his glance stray over the bookshelves and said there was nothing in those books, and what a pity it was. So she just hadn't bothered. But now her feelings are really a bit hurt. Why are the books here more interesting than hers? There's no doubt about it—he really thinks so. Hugo would never say such a thing merely to curry favour.

She is relieved to hear Miriam say:

"Shall we have our lemonade now? It's been ready a long while."

In the next room the table is already laid. Miriam's

mother and grandmother sit down on the sofa with their coffee cups, the others on the chairs opposite, Hugo in the middle, with Miriam and Josephine on either side.

Miriam mixes the lemonade, serves it, and offers them cakes. She is polite, well brought up, just as perfectly behaved as in school. But she doesn't say a word—only "Won't you have some more of this"—or "Please take some more."

It is Hugo who keeps the conversation going. At perfect ease, as if he did it every day, he talks about everything under the sun. Literally—because the conversation begins with how to dig for potatoes and ends with air travel.

Again and again Miriam's mother tries to draw her into the conversation, but it's difficult. And Josephine, too, holds her tongue. Both of them sit there, silent as a couple of fish.

"You've been in an aeroplane, Miriam," the mother says. "Can't you tell us about it?"

Miriam shakes her head.

"Why not?"

Silence.

"I can understand," says Hugo. "It's easier to give a speech about something you *haven't* done than about something you have."

Miriam throws him a hasty glance.

"Yes," she says breathlessly, "because then you can

make it up. And no one can say you're lying . . ."

The grandmother and mother exchange looks and laugh. But Hugo is serious.

"That's nothing to smile at," he says, "because you're only sure about things you haven't tried. As soon as you're involved yourself it becomes confusing."

"Oh dear," says Miriam's grandmother with a smile. "How hard it must be to be a child!"

Hugo smiles an enigmatic smile.

"Do things get easier, then, as you get older?" he asks. But he neither expects nor gets an answer.

He gets up from the table and says thank you for the lemonade. Josephine does, too. Miriam goes over to a big aquarium at the other end of the room and Hugo follows her. But her mother calls Josephine.

"Won't you come here sometimes and visit Miriam?" she asks. "I think you'd have such nice times together."

"Yes, thank you," says Josephine hastily, looking over towards the aquarium.

"Miriam is too often on her own," her mother says. "She isn't used to being with children of her own age, but once she gets going she's very gay and jolly."

"Yes," says Josephine. And looks anxiously towards the other end of the room.

"Well, then, come whenever you like."

"Thank you," says Josephine, and runs over to the others.

She hears Hugo asking what the different fish are called. And Miriam gives the same full answers as always—as if the question were being put to her in school. But her voice is lighter now.

She stands leaning her head against the aquarium: the green water throws reflections in her face, and the light falls on her hair, which shines and gleams like silk. She looks like some mysterious being from another world. A strange magic hovers around her. For a moment she raises her head and looks at Josephine. The look in her dark eyes is expressionless. But Josephine feels uncomfortable. It makes her shy, embarrassed, confused. She feels so childish in front of Miriam!

She wonders whether Hugo does, too, but just now he only has eyes for the fish.

"They're terrific," he says. "Are they yours?"

"I got them on my birthday."

"That must have made you happy," says Josephine. But she feels at once how childish it sounds; she blushes and regrets having opened her mouth.

Miriam doesn't reply immediately. She raises her middle finger to her mouth and thoughtfully bites a nail.

"They're a bit quiet," she says.

"You don't talk very much, either," says Hugo.

Thoughtfully, Miriam contemplates her nails, chooses her third finger, puts it to her mouth, and bites.

"If what you really want are some birds in a cage that can twitter, maybe you find fish in an aquarium a bit sad and silent . . ."

A flash passes through Hugo's eyes, his eyebrows shoot up. He gives Miriam a quick look of unaffected astonishment.

Josephine sees from his face that he understands something which she can't—but which Miriam can. They start talking over Josephine's head, not looking at one another but at the fish.

"Of course, they can't shed their feathers," says Hugo.

And she answers:

"No, it isn't so easy when you have scales."

And then they say no more.

Josephine has understood nothing. But in the silence that follows she realizes something instinctively: Miriam isn't a child. Her chubby hand is childish. But she isn't.

II

S NOW IS the strangest thing. Especially when it first falls. It had been snowing all night. In the morning the whole world is white, and the sun shines on the snow. At school, the teacher lights a candle.

Miriam has the most beautiful fur hat. It's blue, with woolly white fur all round her face. Everyone admires it—unwillingly—from a distance. But Josephine forgets who the hat belongs to. Fur has a mysterious power over her: she must stroke it. At break she goes up to Miriam and runs her hand over the fur. It's so soft and thick, so incredibly lovely, that she forgets herself. Miriam stands quite still, her face half averted. Wordlessly, Josephine strokes the fur, laughing softly to herself, because it's so soft and tickly.

Then Miriam does something unexpected. Suddenly she turns to Josephine, takes off her hat, and holds it out to Josephine.

"You can have it," she says, and runs off.

There stands Josephine, with the wonderful winter cap in her hand, confused, red in the face. Right in the middle of the playground! She hasn't the faintest idea what to do next.

After break is over, she goes to the hook where Miriam's coat is hung and places the hat over it.

But during the next break she sees Miriam walking about bare-headed in the playground. And the same thing is repeated, all day. What on earth should she do?

If she could only talk to Miriam! If it were one of the others, she could go up to her and say: "Here's your hat. Of course you must keep it yourself." But not to Miriam! It's unthinkable. Why? Josephine couldn't say.

Instead, each of them moves about on her own in the playground. Josephine wearing her old cap, Miriam bare-headed. Meanwhile the wonderful hat hangs all by itself on the hook in the corridor. It's enough to drive one crazy!

Josephine hopes Miriam will understand and put on her hat as usual when it is time to go home from school. But no! Off she goes—bare-headed.

Now they've all gone and their clothes too. But

the fur hat still hangs there on its hook, like an ex-
clamation point. Well, it can't just hang there, can it?

In the end, Josephine takes it down, meaning to
run after Miriam. But just as she goes out, she sees
Miriam disappearing into her car. Her mother has
come to fetch her. Josephine stands there at a loss.
What shall she do?

Then Hugo comes running. He's in such a tearing
hurry, the snow flies beneath his boots and he doesn't
even see Josephine. When she calls him, he hardly
has time to stop. No. He's not coming home from

school with her as usual. He can't ride "the monster" in the snow, can he? No, she understands that. But— what about people's mail?

Well—Miriam's mother has offered to drive him around with it in her car. Afterwards he's going to shovel snow for her.

He must run now. They're waiting, he says, and is gone. She turns her back, in order to avoid seeing him get into the car. Not until she hears the engine starting does she turn round and walk out through the school gate.

It is then that she discovers the fur cap in her hand. At least she might have thought of letting Hugo take it with him! Now she'll have to take it home.

Slowly, Josephine walks home. Walks and walks, through the snow, all alone on the road. Everything's so quiet and white it's enough to make one quite scared. Everything's white—even the sky.

Suddenly the whole world seems sad. It didn't this morning. Then the sky was blue, and the snow shone. Now it's cloudy, and the snow just looks cold.

For a brief moment the clouds break. The sun floats up like the face of an anxious child. A second later it sinks again, drowning in clouds. Slowly, snow begins to fall. Josephine feels as if she were walking through nothingness.

The worst moment will be when she gets home and hears everyone ask:

"Where's Hugo?"

And:

"What's that fur cap? Who's it belong to?"

If only she could meet someone on the way! If only something would happen! Something she could talk about when she gets home. Something else—so that they would forget to ask. Her legs feel heavy. She walks and walks. But she meets no one. Nothing happens. It just snows and snows.

Home again. She creeps in, as silently as possible, hangs up her clothes, slips upstairs with Miriam's fur cap. Somewhere she hears voices. Just in time . . . she hides the cap in the depths of her clothes cupboard.

Then she goes down to have tea.

Mama is sitting by the telephone, talking; Mandy has gone shopping in the village. Josephine drinks her tea alone. That's nice, because she can think her thoughts in peace. The tea scalds her tongue, hurting her in more ways than one. If Hugo had been there, they'd have had hot cocoa. Now he must be having cocoa at Miriam's.

Mama comes, and Josephine makes haste to eat up. They talk about the snow and school. She asks Josephine about her lessons. She doesn't seem to notice that Hugo isn't here today. Relieved, Josephine answers her questions. She keeps talking, and all's well. Mama doesn't ask. So Josephine hurries up to her own room. Have to do my homework, she says. But she forgets her exercise books in the hall.

After a while Mama comes by and sees them. She calls out to Josephine, asking how she's managed to do her homework without her books.

Getting no answer, she is on the verge of coming up with them, when Mandy comes in, back from the village. What luck!

For now Josephine is sitting in her room unable to talk or answer questions. Her face is so red and wet that she can't show herself. Mama calls again but gets no answer. Josephine just goes over to the door and locks it.

Then she washes her face and calms down. She creeps down the stairs to fetch her books.

Just as she's slipping through the hall, she hears Mandy say to Mama:

"I saw Hugo in the village. He was busy shovelling snow with that little Miriam girl."

And Mama answers:

"So that's why Josephine looked so strange! I thought something was wrong. But I didn't want to ask her . . ."

Josephine rushes up to her own room again.

There! It's always like that! She looked *strange*, Mama said, though Josephine *knows* she looked just as she usually does. Even if they don't ask you directly, there's simply nothing they don't nose out.

You're never free. They see and guess everything! Isn't there *anything* one can keep to oneself?

Now her mother knows.

And now Josephine is angry.

She locks the door behind her again and takes out Miriam's fur cap. Tries it on. The fur is soft to her touch, but it no longer brings her any feeling of happiness. Besides, she looks silly in it. The white fur looks much prettier against Miriam's dark hair. Miriam is altogether much prettier.

But neither of them—neither Miriam nor Hugo—means a thing to her.

Josephine throws the fur cap aside and goes over to the window.

Outside, it's nearly dark and snowing and snowing . . . brrr, how dismal it seems! She leans her forehead against the window-pane. It's cold. She shivers. Water drips on the window-sill. No, she doesn't care a thing about them any more.

It's quite a while before she looks up again. Then she sees a light coming up the drive. It looks like a star, bobbing between the trees. But her eyes are all hazy. She rubs them, and the star turns into a speck of light. It's coming nearer. And stops beneath her window. She opens it.

"Hello!"

"Hello!"

Silence.

"Finished shovelling snow?"

"Yes. Easy as pie."

"Really?"

Silence.

"Like to come in?"

"They're waiting with the car."

"Oh."

Silence.

"It's snowing . . ."

"Yes."

"Well, I'd best be going . . ."

But still he goes on standing there. He holds up his stable lantern, so that its light falls on his face. In the circle of light the snowflakes whirl.

"I've been thinking about what I would give you, Josephine," he says. "Now I know what it's to be. But it will take some time."

She nods.

" 'Bye then."

" 'Bye."

The speck of light vanishes again into the darkness—and turns into a star.

12

IT'S SUNDAY and freezing cold outside.

Hugo has to light his stove. He moves about in his kitchen, doing odd jobs. Today he's not going down to the village. He's busy at home.

First he puts the cat out, and she vanishes with her tail in the air. Next he washes up and throws the water out of the window.

Then he sees some elk waiting. They stand pressing their noses against the fruit trees, as usual. He hurries upstairs and fills a basket with apples.

As he comes out, the big antlered animals stand in absolute stillness. They never come to meet him, just stand there motionless, sniffing and waiting, until he's poured out the apples on the snow under the trees. And then they only begin to eat when he's taken out his little flute and starts to play to them.

They like music with their meals. The little piece they like is his favourite, too. He learned it on the radio. Usually it's played twice a year. It's in a symphony that has a chorus at the end. The person who made it up is called Beethoven. Hugo picked out the notes all by himself. First he sang them. Then he picked them out on his flute.

Hugo thinks they contain everything that's important on earth. All living creatures can understand them. The male elk lifts up his great antlers and listens, the cow turns her head to one side and looks at him, the calf drops his hoof.

He takes a turn round them; then, still playing, he goes back into his cottage.

When he enters he opens the door of the stove and lays a couple of sticks on the fire. Then he tends to his spider jars. He studies a drawing of a spider's web he has drawn, then puts it aside. He sits down and ponders.

On the table in front of him lies a letter. From the newspaper. They want him to write something. Anything he likes—about spiders, by all means. In fact, spiders seem to interest them most.

He takes out his pencils, sharpens them carefully, takes a large sheet of wrapping-paper, and begins up at the top.

Now and again he pauses for thought. Then he walks about the kitchen. Stopping in front of the window, he takes another turn, comes to a standstill in front of the large chest-of-drawers, then contemplates the picture above it. In the picture, a frigate is under sail, proud and beautiful, her sails bellying in the wind. The sea swells in great rollers, green as the forest, the spray flying like thistledown at midsummer. It's a lovely picture. He has carved and painted the frame himself. On the white space under the ship are some foreign words: *para terras longinquas.* One doesn't need to know what the words mean to understand them. One has a sort of intuition . . . One need only look at the sails and the foam round the bows.

told me about them. I shall now repeat her words
for you. My cradle hung from a big iron hook in
the ceiling. The hook is still there. It is between
the window and the stove. I can see it from here,
where I sit writing. It is old and rusty. The cradle
has gone now. Under the ceiling there are always
lots of spider's webs. My mother took them away.
Unnecessary work, it was. Because every night new
spider's webs came. When she tore the webs down
I cried and got angry. So she let them be. And
often she found a big spider clambering over my
face. It strayed over my forehead or hands. Then
I would laugh, she said. I can't remember this. But
the webs on the ceiling have always been the most
beautiful things I know. When the sun shines and
glimmers in them. Or when they are red from the
glow of the fire. Or at night, when it's dark in the
room and only the spider's webs on the ceiling are
gleaming in the moonlight. It's quite unnatural,
how beautiful it is. Then you think you are dreaming. Maybe you are. I dream quite a lot at night.
When I got bigger, my father began telling me
stories about the spiders. He knew other stories,
too, but the ones I liked best were about spiders.
They are so very much like the people down in the
village, my father used to say. In their way of
living, not in their appearance. My father says
that people, too, spin invisible webs. When we

walk through the village, he and I, he has a habit
of whispering that here begins Shopkeeper Berg's
huge web. It is a huge big web, which most people
are struggling in. But Shopkeeper Olsson's is
much smaller. Not many people get caught in it.
But we did, once. Anyway, Olsson's web has been
torn down. When we got to the church and chapel,
Father said that these were two splendid strong
webs. And magnificent to look at, too. Though we
haven't been caught by them, you and I, he said.
But there's the school, and that's not a bad web,
either. And there you'll be caught, he teased. As a
matter of fact I have been, together with all the
other young spiders. But I'll find a way out one
day. In this world there are webs everywhere. And
everyone struggles in each other's webs. It's not
always so easy to say who is the spider and who
is his victim. Anyone who writes a book spins a
web. Anyone who reads a book is struggling in a
web. But no one knows about this, says my father.
That's why so many people think spiders are nasty
horrible things. They believe these creatures bode
ill. They are only reminded of themselves. Though
this is something they don't understand. It is
interesting. One does not know whether one is
spinning webs for others or for oneself. That's
something you find out afterwards. Writers of
books, for example, often get hopelessly caught in

13

ALMOST every day Hugo shovels snow at Miriam's house. Then he often disappears into the library. He takes down book after book from the shelves and carefully leafs through them. But he does not say what he is looking for.

Sometimes Miriam comes in and keeps him company. She can sit silently for long periods at a time. That's something Josephine can never do. They aren't a bit alike.

One day Miriam's granny comes in and asks Miriam to fetch her shawl from a room upstairs. Then something odd happens. Miriam is scared out of her wits. Her eyes wide with terror, she stares at Hugo. From the fear on her face you'd think she'd been struck by some unimaginable disaster.

"Will you come, too?" she asks.

"Yes."

They go up. Outside the door of the room where the shawl is hanging, Miriam stops to pluck up courage. She is pale and breathing hard. This arouses Hugo's curiosity.

"Are there ghosts in there?"

She shakes her head.

"Worse, much worse," she whispers.

At last, her eyes wide with fright, she opens the door.

It is a lovely old-fashioned room, with white furniture; it is lighter and brighter than any of the other rooms in the house. It's hard to see what could be frightening about it. But Miriam, as if hypnotised with horror, stands staring at one particular spot. He follows her gaze. And the sight nearly takes his breath away.

The wall between the windows is completely covered by a painting of the sea—grey and threatening. The sky above is threatening, too. It's blowing a full gale, and ships, their sails torn by the gale, are being tossed about like walnut shells. Bewitched, Hugo stares at the picture. In its strange way it is wonderfully beautiful.

"Don't look at it," whispers Miriam. "Come, I've found the shawl."

"Is it that picture you're frightened of?"

She nods. The sea scares her to death, she says. Just to look at the picture is enough to make her feel she's drowning. She can be sitting in some other room. Suddenly, she gets it into her head that the sea is coming alive, pouring in through all the doors and all the rooms, drowning the whole house.

"But there's something else, too," she confesses. "There's a horrible book in this room."

"Where?"

"Do you really dare to look at it?"

Yes. He dares.

Beneath the picture stands a little bookshelf with glass doors. With a quivering finger she points at one of the books.

"Read!" she whispers. "Do you see what's written on the cover?"

Hugo reads: *Dead Souls.*

Miriam trembles. She tells him the book is about all the people who have been drowned at sea. It's *their* dead souls that are meant!

Hugo says nothing. But he opens the glass door and takes out the book. His courage is more than she can understand. He even sniffs at the book. She takes a step away from him.

"It's an old book," he says.

"The picture's old, too," she whispers. "So they've been dead an awfully long while."

Hugo begins to leaf expectantly through the book.

"It's not impossible," he says, "that there are souls hidden in this book. But somehow I don't think they're dead ones. Your granny talks about books having souls . . . Haven't you noticed?"

She shakes her head. It's monstrous to see Hugo standing there, turning over the book's pages, just as if it were any old book. Now he's even reading it!

"What does it say? Do the souls howl? Do they scream?"

"No, not so far as I can see, they don't. There's something here about a puppy who's got fleas on his stomach. He scratches with his paws and gives out a whining sound, it says. Then they have to comb it, and the fleas disappear."

Miriam looks sceptical and takes a quick look inside the book. It's as Hugo says. They turn over more pages, in either direction, but find nothing at all about dead sailors. Queer. Where did she get the idea? She can't say. She just believed the book to be about dead sailors because it was underneath the picture.

But suddenly she gives a cry:

"A flea! Do you see? There?"

A little black creature is moving at top speed across the yellowing page.

A blissful smile spreads across Hugo's face.

"At last!" he says. "Thanks very much indeed, Miriam. I didn't see the little beauty . . . I wasn't paying attention."

In a flash he has taken out a glass jar and caught the little creature.

Miriam begins to laugh. A low relieved laugh.

"But—it's half-witted, calling fleas dead souls. Authors must be mad."

"I don't know," says Hugo honestly.

She throws a scrutinizing glance at the picture.

"One doesn't know what to believe," she says.

Hugo stuffs the jar with "the little beauty" into his pocket. He looks thoughtful. He must go now.

She follows him out, waits while he puts his skis on. She is unusually sociable.

"Did you say Granny talks about the souls of books?" she asks him.

"Yes."

"Poor Granny . . . someone ought to tell her . . . they're only fleas . . ."

Miriam looks secretive. She gives another low laugh.

"But we're not telling, are we?"

"Not on your life," Hugo promises, and he flies away across the snow on his skis.

When he gets to the vicarage, he asks Josephine if he can speak to her father. Yes, he can. Papa-Father is at home. He needs only to step inside. With a solemn expression on his face, Hugo goes straight up to the vicar and hands him the glass jar.

"Now I've really got one," he says triumphantly. "Like I promised. It's yours."

"My word," says Papa-Father. "A book scorpion! I'd never have believed it! Where on earth did you find him?"

"That's a secret . . . A bit complicated, because someone thinks it's a book soul, you see. And another that it's a flea. It's best if she does, because then she won't be frightened of dead souls any more. But the other one mustn't know anything about this, you see, because she's scared to death of fleas. That's why I can't tell you where I found it."

"I understand," says Josephine's father.

That is to say, he understands it's something he doesn't understand. He's a wise man.

Josephine doesn't say a word about all this, though she looks seriously at the creature in the jar.

"He wants some sugar, I think," she says.

"No, no, he doesn't want sugar. What he wants is bookworms. You've got millions of them in your books, and they're going to eat up every book you've got, right through from end to end, if you don't plant a book scorpion among them."

Now they let the creature loose on a large sheet of white paper. It runs backwards as fast as it runs forwards. On its front legs it has little claws.

"In the old days they thought he was a little scorpion. That's why they call them book scorpions. But they belong to the spider family really," Hugo explains proudly, on behalf of these animals. He catches the insect again.

"Have you got a book called *Dead Souls*?" he asks.

Yes, they have. They pick it out and Hugo examines it for bookworms. He finds some. The book is an old one.

"Then we'll plant this one here, so he can feel at home," says Hugo, pleased; and he carefully puts the creature down on a yellowing page. For a moment it stands quite still, waving its claws threateningly. Then it scuttles away across the page and disappears inside the book.

"Useful creatures," says Hugo, following it with a tender glance. "I'll see to it that you get some more of them. They're needed here."

Papa-Father looks thoughtful.

"So book scorpions live on creatures who live on

books?" he says. Hugo nods. Josephine's father says with a laugh:

"Almost like us humans, then! After all, we have our critics, who live off the author—who is a sort of creature that lives on books."

"Like bookworms?" Josephine wonders.

"Or book scorpions," says Hugo. And thinks to himself: It's just as his father has always said: the world of spiders and the world of men have a lot in common.

14

WILL THE WINTER ever end?

The snow sweeps across the countryside. It is cold and windy. People have red tips to their noses, and their cheeks glow like coals. The snow gets inside your boots, inside your cap, inside your collar.

"I've had just about enough of this. What I want now is spring," says Hugo.

The wind seizes them. Blinded by the snow, they struggle on.

In the village it's as if all the houses had been rubbed out, as if all noises had been swallowed up. It is deathly still. They hurry into the school-house.

"Is she here yet?" Josephine asks, excitedly.

Hugo nods. The key is in the door. That means the teacher is inside.

"Are you going to speak to her alone?"

"You can come in, too."

They knock on the door.

"Come in!"

The teacher is sitting at the harmonium, dusting it off.

"There's something we wanted to talk about, Miss."

"Oh, really?" says the teacher. "And what can that be?"

"It may seem as though it hasn't much to do with anything," says Hugo, looking seriously at the teacher. "But when one goes to school, one gets sort of mixed up with everything that happens, you see?"

"Of course," says the teacher. "Well, come on then. Out with it."

Hugo throws a hasty glance towards the window. The snow is falling heavily.

"It's about *Thy Bright Sun*," he says.

"I don't understand . . . What do you mean, Hugo?"

"What I mean is, one oughtn't to talk without thinking. Well, should one sing without thinking?"

The teacher shakes her head, still not understanding.

Hugo runs his fingers through his hair once or twice, energetically. Then, in a friendly but firm voice, he explains his point of view to the teacher. He

asks her not to get angry; but seeing as how it has
been the depths of winter now for several months, it
does seem a bit silly to stand there "raising a joyful
sound" every morning, giving thanks for a sun that
never puts in an appearance.

"It doesn't make sense," he says. "It seems as if we
just stand there squawking without thinking."

"But after all, it is a morning hymn," says the
teacher. "The sun *has* risen, even if we can't see it."

"I know," says Hugo. "But it seems rather non-
sensical to stand there crowing about a *bright* sun,
when we haven't had a single bright sunny day
since . . ."

"Not since November," Josephine interrupts. "It's
been snowing every day. Spring will never come."

A wrinkle appears between the teacher's eyebrows. She doesn't look angry. Only astonished.

"My dear children," she says. "Surely you don't imagine spring will come quicker if we stop singing *Thy Bright Sun*, do you? I don't understand your line of reasoning."

Josephine looks to Hugo for help. He comes to the rescue. "Josephine means God may not like it. He might think we're sort of nagging him."

"Or being sarcastic," adds Josephine.

"Or else he may realize we're not thinking at all. And that'd be the worst thing in my opinion."

The teacher smiles softly.

"I see," she says, over and over again. "I see . . ."

"And then it gets so monotonous, both for us doing the squeaking and for him who has to listen to the same old tune, morning after morning . . . if you'll excuse my being so blunt about it."

"What you mean is, God may have tired of hearing *Thy Bright Sun*. Is that it Hugo?"

"It's not impossible . . ."

For a while the teacher sits silent. Then she looks at Hugo. The expression on her face is half-laughing, half-serious.

"There are quite a lot of things at school *you've* grown tired of, Hugo. I've understood this for some time now."

He gives her a searching look.

"Since you say so yourself, Miss. Yes. There isn't much variety, no, there isn't. It's spelling, then singing a bit, then adding up some figures or reading a line or two. And then it's spelling again. I know all that by now."

"But the others don't, you see, Hugo. And we have to think of them."

"I haven't said anything else. Only you asked me yourself. And if we could only start the day without those sounds of joy, it wouldn't be so bad . . ."

The teacher doesn't give him any immediate reply. She just sits there with her thoughts. Now and again she shakes her head. Looks out of the window. The snowflakes are as big as children's hands.

"I'll think the matter over," she says.

"That's very kind, I'm sure," says Hugo. "Thanks."

They go towards the door, and the teacher goes back to dusting her harmonium. Then she says:

"I saw what you wrote in the newspaper, Hugo. That was nice, wasn't it?"

"Was it?"

"Yes, I think so."

"But it was all about spiders."

"Yes, I understand they are interesting creatures."

"Now that something's been written in the newspaper about them, yes! But until then no one understood."

The teacher lifts her hand and points to the door.

The school bell rings.

"Tell the others to come in now. It's time to begin."

It is quite a while before all are properly in their seats. Josephine waits with excitement to see what is going to happen.

As the hymn begins, she looks proudly about her. *Praise to the Holiest in the Height* instead of *Thy Bright Sun.* Success!

But the dimwits in the class don't seem to care *what* they are singing. They just wear the same old expressions on their faces as ever. They don't even notice the change.

She transfers her glance to Miriam and realizes that Miriam doesn't know *Praise to the Holiest in the Height*, because her lips are moving quite differently. Luckily, she sings so softly no one in the class notices it. Interested, Josephine stares at her lips and wonders what sort of nonsense she's standing there singing. At length Miriam feels this glance resting upon her and squirms.

During the first break no one goes out. It's so cold that the teacher says they can stay in.

Suddenly Hugo runs off. And Miriam after him. And Josephine. But they don't go together.

Hugo disappears. The others stand by themselves in the big playground. Miriam behind the school. Josephine in front of it.

Josephine feels cold, she's sorry she has come out.

She thinks she'll have to run round the building to get warm again.

In front of the door to the boiler-room stands Miriam. Her head is flung back. Her eyes are shut. And she's catching snowflakes on her tongue. It looks lovely. Without stopping to think, Josephine runs up, stands beside her, and does the same. Neither looks at the other. Or says a word.

The bell rings. Both look up. For a moment their eyes rest on the notice on the boiler-room door: NO ADMISSION FOR UNAUTHORIZED PERSONS.

Miriam makes a snowball and flings it at the notice. Josephine does the same

Then they run on in.

Suddenly, in the afternoon, the snow stops.

Everyone is sitting at his desk, doing writing exercises. There's a vague sound of scratching. Now and then someone scrapes his foot. The teacher sits knitting. Now and again her knitting needles click. Someone stifles a yawn. Otherwise all is quiet.

Then—suddenly—a sunbeam comes into the room.

It falls at an angle across the blackboard. Everyone looks up. The tulips on the teacher's desk raise their heads slightly, too.

The sunbeam crosses the room, forming a great path of sunlight. Specks of dust shiver and sparkle.

The teacher exchanges a swift glance with Josephine. Then she looks at Hugo.

But he's looking up at the ceiling.

For a moment she thinks he is just pretending—pretending to be unaware of his share in it. Then she realizes he's just on the look-out for a spider's web.

15

ONE DAY in April Miriam's mother comes to the school and hands out invitation cards to the whole class.

"Miriam's going to give a little going-away party," she says.

And that's how they learn that Miriam is leaving.

"Hasn't Miriam told you?" asks her mother, astonished.

They were only staying here for the winter. It was decided from the beginning, she says.

"Really? No, Miriam hasn't said a word."

No. She never does. There she stands, a short distance away from all the others, looking disinterested —as if none of this concerned her. Now and again her mother tries to bring her into the conversation.

But she hardly notices. She looks at her wrist-watch and asks:

"Shouldn't we be going now? Granny's waiting for dinner."

It is Miriam who is hurrying her mother. Usually it's the other way round. Her own going-away party doesn't even interest her!

She's a mystery.

Half a year she's been coming to school, but no one knows her. And she knows no one—except Hugo. And possibly—very slightly—Josephine.

She's incomprehensible!

Why hasn't she even learned the names of her classmates? In the beginning, everyone thought it was conceit. Then they realized it was probably sheer indifference. Such things quite simply don't concern her. Really, she'd be happiest if no one knew her name, either.

For a while they tried to call her Mirry. They thought it might make things easier. But then, for some reason, Hugo intervened.

"Her name's Miriam," he said.

And so it remained—since it was he who said so.

Josephine has a rather bad conscience on Miriam's account. Or, more exactly, on her mother's account. She knows perfectly well Miriam's mother would have liked them to become friends. But they never did. Why not?

Sometimes Josephine has wanted it—sometimes she hasn't. And now, soon, it'll be too late.

Sometimes she can't stand the sight of Miriam. She's been so jealous of her that she's . . . well, she's ashamed when she thinks of it. Every nasty thought you can think of has passed through her head.

Miriam likes Hugo. He's the only one in the school she cares about. And Hugo likes her, too. Not that Josephine has ever asked him. But she knows it. He doesn't think she's strange, as all the others do.

If it comes to that, though, he never finds it impossible to understand anyone. Or even hard. And he's never sorry for anyone, either—least of all himself.

But there's something peculiar about Miriam.

He behaves differently when he's with her. And that's why Josephine has been so madly jealous. She's been jealous of everything about Miriam, her hair, her eyes, her clothes, the black and white checked dresses she wears because her daddy had died. Yes, she's even been jealous of her *because* her daddy's dead, as Hugo's mother is. Because they can share their mourning. And Josephine hates herself for this.

Josephine is sitting at home in her room, contemplating her invitation card. It has violets on it, because spring has come. Miriam's mother or granny must have written it. Certainly not Miriam . . .

Fancy her moving away . . .

In a way it makes her sad. In another it doesn't.

Josephine stares at the card but feels no real joy over the party. She knows Miriam doesn't, either. But that's not why she feels sad. The whole thing's as queer as can be.

Could things have been different between them?

Did Miriam want to be friends with her, in spite of everything?

Suddenly she gets up and goes over to the cupboard. She opens the door and takes out a shoe box, which is tucked away at the back.

In it are all the things she's been given by Miriam.

Gloomily she lifts the lid and looks at them.

There's the fur cap. The white fur is still just as clean and lovely. She hasn't worn it. Nor any of the other things. And Miriam has never asked her why.

There is the big black silk bow that Miriam had worn once under her white collar. Josephine had chanced to remark how pretty it was, how lovely and shiny it looked.

Miriam had taken it off at once and given it to her. And then run off, before Josephine could say a word! Just as she did with the fur cap.

After that, Josephine should have known better than ever to say there was anything of Miriam's she liked. But she hadn't stopped to think.

That's why the box also contains a bracelet. It is a

silver chain, with white china hearts on it. And a brooch in the shape of a little lizard.

On Miriam these things had positively shone, so that Josephine had regarded them as little miracles. But as soon as she got them herself, all the shine had gone out of them.

One by one she picks up the objects.

Was it Miriam who gave them their mysterious glimmer? Now Josephine just thinks they're sad to look at. She wants to cry. Her conscience throbs.

Did Miriam give them to her to make her happy?

Because she likes Josephine? Why did she run off, then, and never let her thank her? Afterwards, it was impossible to bring up the subject.

Only once did Josephine manage to get a word in. That was when she got the bracelet. Then she said she didn't like taking it away from Miriam.

But Miriam gave her such a queer look, with something so ice-cold in it. She said that if Josephine didn't want the bracelet, she could throw it away. She herself didn't have any more use for it. Her voice sounded hard.

What could one reply to that? And Josephine didn't want to throw away the bracelet.

Here at home no one knows anything about all these things. No one has even seen them. She's scared they might. Even though they were presents, she still feels like a thief. Because it must all mean something, she doesn't understand what. Maybe she'll never understand.

Many of the others had said nice things about Miriam's possessions. But she never gave them anything. Only Josephine. If they knew, they'd be dreadfully jealous. But it always happened when no one was looking.

If only Josephine could throw the whole lot into the fire . . . Get rid of it all.

But that's easier said than done. The memory

would remain. And her guilty feelings would only be worse.

Will she have to carry these things around with her for the rest of her life? Without understanding why she was given them? Without daring to get rid of them? Just for Miriam's sake?

16

HUGO ISN'T going to Miriam's party.

Even when he got his invitation card, he looked dubious. The next day he tells Miriam he doesn't think he'll come.

"My dad and me, see, we never go to parties. They're not for us."

"No," Miriam answers.

"I don't feel like it . . ."

"Nor me."

She looked pleased. Not at all sorry he has said no.

There's a lot of whispering about it. But it can't be helped. His refusal draws a certain amount of suppressed attention—suppressed because it's Hugo. Otherwise it would be a different story. After all, it does sound a bit strange—not giving any excuse. You could be ill, or invited somewhere else. Something of that sort. Just saying openly it's because you don't want to . . .

In fact, the one is as unheard of as the other: imagine not wanting to! And then just saying so!

And Miriam . . .

She says she doesn't want to go, either. And looks pleased when her guests say no. Not very polite, is it?

Everyone is pleased that he or she knows better. But they feel sorry for her mother, having such a daughter! So ungrateful! They would be so *much* nicer about it. They sigh. They can understand that poor mother's feelings only too well . . .

It is a wonderful party—a superior party. Everyone has a party dress on. Many have bought new ones in town. And shiny shoes and stockings. Hair freshly washed, curls, bows, jewellery, and perfume.

The boys are wearing suits and white shirts. When they arrive, their hair is all plastered down with water. But this passes over. Soon they look the same as usual.

Josephine is wearing a grey skirt and green angora sweater, which she thinks is lovely. That is, until she notices the others' disapproving glances.

Two girls are standing in front of the mirror. One is saying to the other:

"Haven't you heard it's *rude* to wear a skirt and sweater to a party?"

"Of course! You just *have* to wear a dress at a *party*."

"Imagine some people not knowing . . ."

Then Miriam's mother comes in—also in a skirt and sweater!

"Is it me you're talking about?" she asks, merrily.

The lobes of their ears turn red. They say:

"Of course not . . ."

As a matter of fact, they were talking about certain *other* people. Which is why they throw a surreptitious glance in Josephine's direction. But Miriam's mother just laughs and shakes her head at them.

"What funny little things you are," she says. "Don't you see that in this house we wear exactly what we like? I don't think Miriam has even changed her dress . . ."

No. So they see. There she stands, wearing one of her black and white checked dresses. It's a fact! And woollen stockings, too! It makes one positively embarrassed on her behalf. *Really*, one just has to pretend not to see!

They've scraped together a farewell gift for her. She gets some flowers and a book. You can see it written all over her that she hadn't expected anything. She gets all embarrassed—and *curtsies* as she thanks them. They have to pretend not to see that, either! Though that little nitwit Josephine, of course,

has to go and curtsey back. Which one can't help gig-
gling at a little, *after all*! For, *really*, it isn't *her* party,
is it?

Miriam's mother and grandmother follow them
into the dining-room, and then disappear. Miriam is
left alone with her guests.

Going over to the end of the dining-table, she
stands looking out across its surface—one endless
gleam of glass and china, silver and candles. It looks
like a fairy-story ship. The neatly folded napkins are
like little sails. Miriam thinks it's rocking. Unlike
Hugo, she doesn't like ships. They remind you of the
sea, which people get drowned in.

She takes a firm grip on the table end.

Meanwhile, all the others stand shyly along the
sides of the room. No one wants to be the first to sit
down.

"Please sit down," they hear Miriam say, in her
hostess voice. "There are place cards to tell you
where to sit."

They all rush forward at once, like pirates board-
ing a ship. There is a moment's confusion until everyone has found his or her place.

The hostess sits down last of all. On her right sits
Josephine.

Which is why Josephine is served first.

No one says a word. Everyone looks at her. How
will she behave?

The candle flames burn stiff and still, expectantly.

A housemaid in black with a white apron and a little lace cap—just as a parlour-maid should be—puts down the potatoes on Josephine's right and serves the meatballs from her left—just as a parlour-maid should.

Josephine gets all confused. To gain time she turns her back on the maid and helps herself first to the potatoes. The maid waits patiently.

A murmur passes across the table. The candle flames tremble with indignation.

"There! Did you see? She took the potatoes before the meat . . ."

Josephine knows perfectly well what a monstrous crime she is committing. Always making mistakes, even though she knows they're mistakes. It's inevitable, a law of nature. Something inside her always gets jammed.

She blushes. Goes hot all over. Her angora sweater pricks and tickles.

Terrified, she stares at the round meatballs. As she tries to pick them up, one of them starts rolling away. Rolls off the dish. Down on to the tablecloth. On to her skirt. On to the carpet. Two more follow.

All around her there's a tremendous sighing and fluttering. But she is no longer really conscious of what is happening. In a sort of fog she sees the maid picking up the meatballs. With a white napkin the maid wipes the tablecloth, her skirt, and the carpet, smiles at Josephine and says it doesn't matter at all.

"Pass the potatoes," says someone in an audible hiss—someone who knows how things should be done at a party.

"One has to think of the other guests, too . . ."

"Yes, *really*. Not only oneself!"

It dawns on Josephine that it is she they are referring to. Panic-stricken, she searches around for the potatoes. But then, firmly and decisively, Miriam grabs them and helps herself. She places three big potatoes on her own plate. A deathly silence falls. Miriam puts the potatoes back where they were before. The candle flames are petrified with horror.

Josephine takes the potatoes and hands the dish to her neighbour. Then she looks at Miriam, who is staring impassively across the table. At this moment no one knows what she is thinking. She takes the lemonade bottle and, calm as can be, fills her own glass to the brim. And drinks. Before her guests.

She looks at them over the rim of her glass. In the depths of every eye she sees a tiny piece of glittering ice. No one dares say a word. *Really*! There sits their hostess, guzzling lemonade, all on her own! Without offering it to anyone else!

Then Josephine, suddenly reckless, grabs the bottle, pours herself some lemonade and swallows the lot at a gulp. Again Miriam fills her own glass. Aghast, the others just sit and stare. Miriam stares

back defiantly. Then, with an impatient bang, she puts down her glass.

"There's heaps of lemonade," she says. "Why don't you all help yourselves? You don't expect me to go running round the table, do you?"

Miriam—the perfect Miriam! Her mother should just see her now! Her hostess face has disappeared. Surely she must be the oddest person in the whole world.

As at a given signal, and in a way relieved, they all grab for the lemonade bottles. And suddenly everyone becomes natural. There's no one to try and impress any longer. By the time the ice-cream and cake come to the table, all instructions received at home have been utterly forgotten. They heap them

on their plates, each selfishly eyeing the other to see
how much he or she has taken.

"You've got more than me . . ."

"No, I haven't!"

"Yes, you have!"

"You're lying. I haven't. But you . . ."

Miriam, with her unfathomable glances, surveys
them all.

"Take it easy, you little beasts," she cries. "There's
more in the kitchen."

Josephine is chasing candyfloss around her plate.
Now and then she gives Miriam an ecstatic look of
delight; but Miriam doesn't return it. In fact, she
pays no particular heed to anyone. Just goes on ob-
serving them all out of her strange glittering eyes.

At the other end of the table two people are fighting over a marzipan rose.

"Leave that rose alone!" shouts Miriam. "Hero is to
have that!"

Hero is the huge dog. Hearing his own name, he
stalks over, majestic and serious. Someone throws
the rose to Miriam, who immediately lets it vanish
into Hero's vast jaws. Like a drop in the ocean. Hero
looks around hungrily. At once everyone begins
feeding him icing and candyfloss, until the maid
comes in and leads him out:

"Too many sweet things make his eyes bloodshot,"
she says.

As they get up from the table, they compete to blow out the candles. The wax sputters and splashes. All over the table. A perfect feast of wax!

Now they are all so full that they just drop limply into sofas and armchairs. They all gobble sweets so as to be able to carry on.

Miriam has her hostess face on again.

"We'll have a fish-pond afterwards," she informs them politely, putting on a record. A whole heap of records is lying on the table. She says they can play any they like. Then she disappears. Unnoticed. Everyone talks at the same time. They fight over which record to play. No one even notices Miriam's absence.

Except Josephine.

After a while she goes and looks for her. A silly thing to do, maybe, but she does it, even so.

It is a big house, terribly lonely everywhere. All the doors are standing open, and in every room lights are burning. Not under the ceiling. Just little lamps, here and there, in front of mirrors, on chests-of-drawers and tables.

Now she has crept upstairs. No sign of anyone, anywhere, though in every room hangs a faint aroma of soap or perfume—as if someone had just gone out of it. She doesn't know where Miriam's room is. One of the doors is closed. Perhaps it's there? Inside, all is quiet as can be. Not a sound.

For just a moment the thought flashes through Josephine's mind that she has been wandering among these rooms through all eternity—that the party is over, and everyone has gone home. Perhaps she has been bewitched? Become invisible? No one sees her, and she sees no one. Perhaps she'll never get out again? Has she become a ghost? Is she condemned to wander about in these strange rooms for ever and ever, through all eternity?

Suddenly, seized with panic, she turns and runs. She finds the stairs and dashes down again to the others. In the dining-room music is playing, and there's a great hubbub of voices. But no Miriam.

Josephine calms down. She goes back through the house again.

In one of the rooms there is a tiled stove. It looks like a white castle. Its brass doors are open, and inside the embers of a fire are still glowing. For a moment she sits down on the edge of a chair. It's nice in here. Blue flowers are glowing in the windows. Somewhere an invisible clock is ticking secretively.

She gets up and walks about in the room.

Outside it is dark. If you look out you see part of the village, black gardens and dark fields. Here and there lights are burning. You can see the roof of the house where Karin lives.

The stars are gleaming. Those near the horizon

seem closer to the earth. Just above are the most ter-rifyingly distant ones of all.

A large mirror shines like a sea on the wall. How little she looks! Round her neck Josephine has a sil-ver chain, with a big amber oval pendant. All light seems gathered in that amber drop, which shines secretly in the green mirror.

The carpets are so soft, you don't hear anyone coming.

Suddenly, Miriam is standing beside her. They stand awhile, silent, looking askance at their own re-flections. Motionless as two statues. Without looking at one another.

At length Miriam's dusky voice is heard:

"Dark hair is prettier than fair."

But she means the opposite. And Josephine knows it. She answers:

"No, fair hair's prettier than dark."

Each of them gives a sigh of contentment, not taking her eyes off her own image.

Miriam straightens her hair on the right side. Josephine on the left.

The light in the amber drop keeps watch.

"What's that inside it?" asks Miriam.

"Inside what?"

"Your pendant."

"It's amber."

"It's lovely," says Miriam without looking at it.

Then Josephine knows. For just a tiny moment she doesn't move. Then she takes off her chain and hangs it round Miriam's neck.

Miriam draws a deep breath. Josephine too. Neither of them says a word. All at once, there is no longer any need to explain anything. In the mirror they meet each other's glances. Just a second—no more is needed.

Their eyes are clear as water.

17

MIRIAM has moved away.

So that was that!

Once again her grandmother goes for solitary walks with the big dog. She smiles, just as she always did, straight out into the air ahead of her. She's the same as she always was, yet different.

Nowadays one has to see her through different eyes. Before, she was just the lady with the big dog. Now she's Miriam's grandmother. Such things change one's feeling for people.

Josephine always feels a bit solemn when they meet. And she feels a pang of melancholy.

When Miriam's grandmother catches sight of Hugo she usually stops and begins talking about books. Even if he hasn't read them, he always has an opinion, and he likes discussing things. But he never says a word about the book scorpions—having promised Miriam not to. Altogether there were seven of them that he caught and planted in the vicarage.

Before Miriam left, Hugo gave her a horse that he had carved out of wood. It was the best horse, without a doubt, that he had ever carved. She thought so, too. Sometimes he talks about the horse. But never about Miriam.

One day spring has really arrived. In the spring breeze everything is glittering and fluttering, giving off its perfume. The streams are chuckling.

Just a moment ago they met Miriam's grandmother.

Suddenly Josephine asks:

"Do you miss her?"

"Who?"

"Miriam."

"No—don't think so."

They cross the meadow and the birds twitter so loud that the sun quivers in the air.

"Do *you*?" asks Hugo.

"I don't know. A little, maybe."

The grass glitters so vividly that each blade seems to tremble in the sunshine. Hugo throws himself down full-length, and Josephine sits down beside him. High above the meadow the swallows are hovering. He follows them with his gaze.

"What are you thinking about?" asks Josephine.

"That was a stupid thing to ask, wasn't it?"

She throws him an angry look. But he looks calmly back at her and explains:

"Well, how can anyone say what he's thinking, when there're a hundred things at once going through his head, all in different directions?"

He falls silent, watching the swallows again. Sighs:

"Whether I miss anyone else I couldn't say, but I'm beginning to miss myself."

She laughs.

"Go on! You can't miss yourself, can you?"

But he is serious.

"Of course you can. If you've lost yourself, then you can."

Suddenly, impetuously, he sits up, tugging at the grass with his hand.

"It's school," he says. "I want to study and learn everything. And understand as much as possible. But school gets in the way all the time. I want to go along roads and sail the seas—and I don't want to sit at a desk."

Finding no words, he interrupts himself. Falls awhile into a deep silence.

Then he nods and says:

"That's how it is."

He lies down on his back again and draws a deep breath. His eyes seem bluer than the sky, as he says.

"It's spring. And it's wonderful to be alive."

"Yes."

"But in that case one just has to do something that has some sense to it, surely you can see that . . ."

"Yes."

"It would be childish otherwise."

Suddenly, full of energy, he bounces up.

"Well then, this isn't good enough. I've got a lot to do . . ."

On the edge of the ditch Josephine plucks a couple of wood anemones. She doesn't say anything, she has begun to get used to Hugo by now. She understands something is in the wind.

That day he skips not only the mail delivery but his cup of hot cocoa in the vicarage kitchen as well.

"Now they can fetch their own mail," he says. "It's spring, and people need some exercise."

At the drive their ways part.

She doesn't look back at him. She feels slightly gloomy.

But soon she hears footsteps behind her.

"There's something I forgot. I've got to visit your rubbish heap."

18

HUGO TEARS the page out of the calendar. Turns it over and writes on the back: "Thing for Josephine ready."

Then he pulls out a drawer and throws the paper in among all his other notes. He puts on a clean shirt, packs his knapsack more carefully than usual. On top of all the other items he lays the "thing" and a book about rivers. No school books.

He stands on his porch for a while. It's a lovely morning.

The grass is wet with dew. In the trees one can hear the faint sighing of the spring. Birds are calling. From the depths of the woods comes a sound of axes. It's his father at work. Hugo puts his flute to his lips and blows a signal. His father hears. Whistles back.

Then Hugo puts on his broad-brimmed hat and sets out.

The ground is speckled with white anemones, right up to the school-yard. Under the fruit trees there is a bright blue patch of violets.

His steps make no sound on the soft woodland paths, but sometimes the flapping of wings of big birds up in the treetops can be heard instead. The sunlight filters down between the trees.

A cloud of lily-of-the-valley scent floats by.

Josephine is waiting under the trees. She is sitting on a stone reading. Seeing him, she closes her book and gets up.

"Sit down!" he commands. Astonished, she obeys.

He slings off his knapsack and puts it on the ground. He takes out the "thing", strokes and fingers it a bit, to make sure it is durable and well-made, lovely and smooth. Then he hands it to her.

It is a kaleidoscope.

Josephine looks into it; the first thing she sees is a star, shining in a thousand colours, but immediately afterwards there is a wonderful flower. If she moves it ever so little, the picture changes; it can never be repeated. There can be innumerable stars and innumerable flowers, but they are all quite different from one another.

"What you're seeing now," says Hugo, secretively,

"no one else will ever see." Josephine nods, and the picture is instantly transformed.

She is happy, overwhelmed with surprise.

Hugo has made the kaleidoscope himself, from beginning to end. From a description in an old newspaper.

"There isn't a single rubbish heap in the whole village I haven't investigated, believe me," he says proudly.

"But . . . what did you want to find there?"

"Bits of glass, of course. It had to be glass of every colour."

He laughs and says that now Josephine owns the whole village's discarded rubbish. Turned into stars and flowers by the thousands.

"They've all contributed, see, and that's something you must know."

They laugh delightedly at the idea.

"But you can't give this away," says Josephine.

"Of course I can."

"But you're so fond of it yourself."

"Of course. And that's why I've given it to you."

"Thanks . . ."

"Oh, it's nothing . . ."

"Yes, it is."

"No . . . Anyway, we'd better hurry up, else we'll be late for school."

They get there just as the teacher is sitting down at the harmonium.

"We can sing *Thy Bright Sun*, today, Miss . . ." says Hugo mischievously.

The teacher looks at him.

"Oh, we can, can we?"

"Yes. It would be the most suitable."

"Very well, then, we will."

During the first hour they have drawing and are told to draw spring flowers. On the blackboard the blue anemone, the cowslip, and the lily-of-the-valley stand in all their glory, neatly drawn by the teacher's hand. They can choose. Josephine takes the blue anemone.

But Hugo draws a flag. As usual. By now he has

painted all the flags in the world and is busy with the last; Abyssinia's, because he began at the end of the alphabet with Zambia.

The window is open. The curtain stirs. The sunshine floats through the room and the breeze fans them. Now and then a stray insect buzzes in and out.

When Hugo is finished with his flag, he just sits, deep in thought. He looks out of the window. His eyes shine.

"Haven't you anything to do, Hugo?" asks the teacher.

"Yes, I have," he answers dreamily.

"It doesn't seem so."

To this Hugo makes no reply. He just sits there smiling to himself.

The teacher comes up to him and looks at his flag.

"It's finished now, I see, so you'd better make a start on the spring flowers."

"No, I hadn't." Calmly he shakes his head. "It just isn't possible. Such beauties just can't be copied. You have to look at them carefully and draw them yourself."

With these words he gets up and begins making a tour of his classmates to say good-bye.

Nonplussed, the teacher gapes at him.

"Are you leaving us, then, Hugo?"

"Yes."

"But school isn't over yet."

"There're not so terribly many days left, are there? You'll get along all right without me."

Last of all he goes up to the teacher, takes her by the hand and shakes it.

"Thanks very much, Miss. And good-bye."

He says this with great solemnity. She smiles a little and nods. But she can't find anything to say. Not until he is at the door. Then she asks:

"And where are you going, Hugo?"

Eyes shining, he answers her:

"I'm going to look for a confluence."

"What on earth . . .?"

"That's just what I've got to find out . . . it must be something terrific, tremendous . . ."

For a moment he tries to find words for it; his eyes look far into the distance, seeing something which no one else can see. His voice is low, urgent:

"The waters from two rivers, you see, they join together and flow into one. I've got to find out how it happens . . ."